I0620406

THE
GIN THIEF

EPISODE 1:
BECOMING SCARLET

S.C. BARRUS

To learn more about the author and publisher visit
AwayAndAway.com

Enter one of our monthly book giveaways at
AwayAndAway.com/Giveaway

If you're interested in contacting the author email
scbarrus@awayandaway.com

Copyright © 2014 S.C. Barrus
Published by Away & Away Publishing.

All rights reserved.

ISBN-13: 978-0-9899177-3-5
ISBN: 0989917738

For Tana

CONTENTS

ACKNOWLEDGMENTS

Thanks to the many people who helped make this series possible including kickstarter backers, beta readers, and, of course, Tana Barrus who's been an instrumental part of the creation process.

VICTANIA, 1866

Victania, the most advanced country of the modern age, is the home of a violent class struggle. While advances in technology have enhanced the lives of the upper class, the lower classes fester. Those who cannot find work in the dangerous factories live in squalor: stealing, conning, and whoring to survive.

In this climate, vicious territorial gangs have erupted from the poverty. Among them, one gang stands out as particularly radical: The Scarlets. Made up primarily of women, The Scarlets have fought ferociously to carve out a piece of Victania they could call their own. Now, in the port city of Sundale, The Scarlets have built a small empire run by a mysterious woman known to most only as The Missus.

CHAPTER 1

The room was hazy, smelling thick of lavender, smoke, and licorice. She sat there, upon a mound of pillows threaded with silk strands shimmering from the light of gas lamps on the walls and the red glowing ember before her. Under the ember a sweet herb smoldered and through a coiling tube she drew the smoke into her lungs. I remember her eyes most of all, the way they never left me, always studying.

"You are the wet thing my Candy found on the street, so I hear?" Her voice was a soothing sort of frightening; cold, elegant, seductive, and controlled. The dim light cast upon the lines of her face a faint yellow glow while her more subtle features were cloaked in the darkness.

The walls were ornate, twisting patterns, all shades of red, and in the dim lamp light, they seemed to shift slightly as though the room were breathing. I shivered

— not out of fear, though there was a little of that, but from the cold of the ocean waters still biting into my skin all these hours later.

"Don't be nervous, dear," she spoke with that shallow smile of hers. "You're not the first to arrive in tatters and dirty, stinking the demons out of hell. I don't judge appearances."

Two other women sat upon mounds of pillows on either side of her, each puffing on coiled tubes, each watching me with half interest. To them I was no more than a curiosity one considers for a moment before moving on to the next. But not her, not the woman who'd been introduced to me as The Missus. One of the others — silent until now — snickered as The Missus drew in another breath of smoke with a coy smile.

"That's not entirely true, I suppose," she said. "But you need not worry, dear. Not yet, in any case. As I understand it, you're here seeking entry into our ranks. Very bold. It takes a special kind of girl to become one of us."

I nodded. "Miss Bottoms said—"

"Yes, I know what she told you. I can hear further than you can imagine. Remember that. Miss Bottoms is very good at recruitment but all the girls must meet with my approval before they are granted a bunk. There is more to meet than the simple criteria of what makes a Scarlet, Miss... what was your name again?"

"Over," said I.

"There is more than the simple criteria of what makes a Scarlet, Miss Over. Intriguing name. Yes, you may or may not pass every point of requirement, but there also remains the essence of the girl to take into account. And that is much more — what's the word? — ethereal a thing. It's not something that can be known in a single conversation. Sadly, these days that is all the time I have. So you have two minutes to convince me to carry on a second conversation. You've been in Victania three days now, is that correct?"

"One day," said I, my voice shaking, my accent suddenly sounding very strong. "Bastards locked me up on them docks, I wasn't allowed on Victanian soil. I was trapped there for two days before... before I got away."

"Hmm," she mused, a finger patting her lips, eyes taking in the whole of me as I spoke. "Not an easy task." She turned to the woman on her right, "Most of the immigrants die trying to escape the docks, do they not?"

"I believe many do, the ones who try in any case. Either they're shot by the constables, or they drown. But a few slip through."

"And how did you do it?" she asked me.

"I'll tell ya that when next we speak." I risked a peek into her eyes and found her watching me intently with the faintest flicker of a smile. Again, she tapped her lips.

"Can you speak without an accent?" she asked after a moment.

As she questioned it, I could feel the worry balling up in my throat. "Me accent?" I managed.

"Yes, dear, your accent. I don't expect immediate results, but you would need to matriculate. Could you lose the accent if your standing depended on it?"

"Yes," I replied unsure of myself but utterly desperate. "I think so."

"That bodes well," she said rather sarcastically. "Tell me something about yourself, Miss Over. This is your last chance to woo me."

"I…" I hesitated. I knew I had to say the words; Miss Bottoms had prepared me as she led me by the arm toward this strange, mystical, and dangerous place. "Don't hide from it," she had said. "When you tell her, say it with pride. She can't resist a story of a good killing." While I wasn't sorry for what I had done, I was still regretful. I forced the words out in a spit of a sentence, "I killed…someone. A man."

She watched me for a long moment, inhaling a long draw through the tube, exhaling a twisting serpent of smoke. "Yes," she spoke thoughtfully. "Yes, I can see that you did. You have the look in your eyes. Why did you kill this man of yours?"

"Why?" My chest burned even as my skin

shivered. There was a pit opening inside my heart, a hard thing inside the meat of it rubbing my soul raw. I was not meant to be a killer, but now, in order to survive the night, I was forced to revel in it. "When it comes down to it," my voice tremulous as I realized the truth of my statement, "I killed him over a bottle of gin. Over a bottle of Extra Special Reserve Putrid Gin."

"Truly?" she asked.

I nodded quickly and felt a tear roll down my cheek. I prayed that she could not see it in the dim light.

"An innocent, foreign girl like you killed a man in cold blood over a bottle of Putrid Gin? There's more to this story, isn't there? You do have some spunk. I hate that word, but there you have it." Rising from her seat, she bade me forward with a finger and said, "I want to look into your eyes."

I neared her, pulled in by her gaze. She leaned close to me and I could smell the smoke clinging to her red lips, the smell of perfume and Absinthe; together intoxicating and biting. "Look up," she said with a finger to my chin. The hair on the back of my neck went stiff. "Just here," her eyes were dark and piercing. For a long moment I stood rigid as she stared into me. "Could you do it again?" she whispered. "Could you kill again?"

I swallowed hard and dry. "Could I kill someone?"

"Yes."

"I... I don't..." I hesitated, but the image of my murder filled my view. I remembered him standing over me, I remembered feeling powerless. But then I had found the knife, long and thin, and the knife had found the nape of his neck. Would I kill again? "Yes," I shuddered. "Yes, if..."

"If?"

"In similar circumstances."

"Circumstances are everything," she smiled. "You are beautiful, and there is something in you, something small, but it can be nurtured. Fine. Clean yourself up, get a fresh set of clothes, then go down to The Vexing Valentine. I'll be along. You have my interest for tonight. I'll listen to your story. You are a lucky girl."

CHAPTER 2

A curtain, strung with beads like pearls of colored water, hung gracefully in the doorway. As I parted it and walked through, I felt as though I was rising from the bitter ocean again. I gasped, fell against the wall, clutched to it, hands trembling.

Flashes of the scene erupted in my mind. The knife in my hand — I could feel it still. The blade lost within the collar of his shirt. The weight of him as he fell over me, pinning me to the table. And the blood — how it coated my hand! — dripping upon me, my lungs forgetting to breathe, my heart forgetting to beat. Time had frozen — the beads of blood suspended in the air, my head sick — and even as the hours progressed, that single moment remained forever present within me as if the blood had never ceased to fall.

Startled, I looked about, jolted back to my senses

as if I'd been bludgeoned by a nightstick, but found the source had only been a touch. Miss Bottoms, the girl who had rescued me from a ditch in the cold of the night only hours earlier, watched me carefully with a concerned frown. "You alright?" she asked.

"I don't know." I struggled to right myself, my heart pounding so hard I could feel the blood pulsing in my arms. "I feel anxious," my voice shook, "unbound, unhinged. I don't know."

"Yes," she said knowingly. "That does happen from time to time." Wrapping an arm over my shoulder, she guided me down the hall. "You're in it now," she said. "Best to find your footing quick. Though I have to say, you did me well in there."

I nodded and walked alongside her. It wasn't long ago I had found myself frozen numb from ocean water and autumn air. All I had wanted then was sleep, even if it meant the death of me. That night, when I opened my eyes and found her, Miss Bottoms, crouching over me, wisps of curly brown hair framing her pleasant face, I thought for a moment that I had died and that she was an angel. But here, now, in this hall, the ceiling so high it might as well have been the night sky, I could see the hard edges around Miss Bottoms pleasant features.

"I listened in on your conversation," she said. "You remembered the points I told you. You have got her interest. Made me glad I brought you along.

Most girls we send straight to their bunks, but you, I have a good feeling about you. Next comes the difficult part: you must woo her. Are you listening? Because this is important."

I nodded, but even then I hadn't the mind to understand my situation clearly. The week previous had been an assault of unfortunate, degrading, and violent events against me. In short order I simply began to follow the path of least resistance. Somehow that path had led to me swimming for my life in the ocean and freezing half to death in a ditch. But both were easier than the alternatives. This now, with these self-assured women, this was the simplest path to tread.

"Good," said Miss Bottoms as we walked down the drafty hallway. "There's the first rule, to listen, and you better learn it right quick. Things change in a flash around here and if you're not on your toes you will be left behind. Especially because you're new. Well you're not even new yet. Not even an understudy — that's what we call initiates, remember that. So it behooves you to pay double attention. You're entering a new world within a new country. That's double duty for you. It can be marvelous but it can also be torturous if you're not careful. Understand?"

I nodded. The truth was, I didn't understand. Miss Bottoms had saved my life, fed me, offered me shelter, asked my story, and then brought me here to meet The Missus, but I didn't know her. These women spoke with authority but all of it seemed so strange. Even so, I never hesitated when Miss Bottoms asked me to follow her, nor when she told me to tell The Missus of the man I had killed. When I had told Miss Bottoms of my murder, I cried, but when I told The Missus, I felt almost relieved. The feeling was coming back to my toes bit by painful bit. That too was a relief.

"Excellent," said Miss Bottoms. "When you tell her your story you'll have her strict attention for about five minutes. After that it all depends on you. But she appreciates the art of a good tale so spin it proper. Too short and she'll be disappointed, too long and she'll grow weary. If you've got to embellish a bit, do so. But don't outright lie. She'll catch you if you do. Just don't make her regret listening to you. Understand? That's the quickest way to disappear."

"Disappear?"

"Yes," she pulled me in tight against her, pressed her forehead against mine and looked me in the eyes. "Exciting, isn't it, darling? You're walking along the knife blade now." Crinkling her nose as she caught a whiff of me, she let go and started off down the hall again. "We need to take care of that smell. Come on. Don't get left behind. By the by, what did you think of her?"

"Her?" I asked hardly able to think.

"The Missus."

I hesitated. "I don't know." I wiped my wrist indelicately across my running nose, the smell of my own hand wriggled through me in a disgusting waft. I shuddered and swallowed back tears of frustration and humiliation.

"She's a great woman," said Miss Bottoms decidedly as she led me round a corner. We walked along a hall passing a few well-dressed girls. They're eyes lingered on me as we passed, telegraphing the sentiment, 'You don't belong here.'

"Without The Missus, do you know what we girls would be?"

I decidedly clenched my jaw, fixing my eyes on the ground as we passed the girls.

"What do poor women do where you come from?"

"Where I come from," I whispered. "They sit around home and take care of their dyin' Da."

"That's oddly specific," said Miss Bottoms with a raised brow. "I take it, that's about you. If your father's dead, that's perfect. The Missus will eat that up. She loves dead fathers. But when you tell her the story, it'll be in your favor to leave out the sentimentality.

"In any case," she continued, "Victania is a different world. The poor girls struggle day by day.

The monarchy doesn't care about them; neither do the constables, nor those in any position of power. Except to exploit them anyway. The girls with a bit of luck become factory workers, fingers broken, while breathing in that horrid smoke, the foremen looking down at them as if they're machines. Then they'd die young, tired and exploited. Except *we're Scarlets* which means we're headstrong. We'd be alone, struggling to get by in the streets, ending up jailed, dead, or whoring. But The Missus, she's changed all that.

"Now there are two little pockets she has set up kip, this one in Sundale, the other in Goldengress. She has flipped the world upside down. When you're in here, inside these walls or in our territory, the world bows to us. And if they don't we teach them to, doesn't even matter who they are. The barmy Queen herself walks down our streets and I'll be the one waiting for her to bow. Understand?"

I nodded.

"In here," she said, motioning to a door. A warm cloud of steam rolled out of it and into the hall smelling richly of soap. It was an over-sized bathing room filled with two rows of large steaming wooden tubs. Through the hazy air I saw the skin of four girls wearing naught but the suds of soap. The younger two, roughly aged in their twenties, quit their chattering when they caught sight of me. The older two, who appeared to be in their thirties or forties, lifted their heads from their relaxation.

Nervously I stood within the doorway, my feet unsure. I felt Miss Bottoms' hand on the small of my back as she gently guided me in. Stiffly, I stood in the center of the room, unable to raise my eyes from the damp floorboards.

"What sewer did you pull that creature out of?" asked one of the younger girls. "You sure you're in the right place, love?"

I kept my eyes on the ground, my jaw clenched tight. In the village I was raised in, I was not one to suffer ribbings lightly but here I was an outsider.

"She looks like a drowned rat, doesn't she?"

"Come on," said Miss Bottoms, "off with your clothes, then. We haven't got time to dawdle."

My eyes refused to look at the other girls as I stripped my clothing.

"What are you waiting for, hop in. A bath will do you good."

My hands were dirty, my fingernails still lined with the brown stains of blood. My cheeks burned with embarrassment. But as Miss Bottoms showed me the pump and the steaming water began pouring in, searing my frozen toes so sweetly, I was almost able to ignore their comments entirely and simply melt away in the water.

But when I heard one say in a voice I was meant to hear, "Candy, did you have to bring this one in? I can smell her stink from here. What kind of scatty hobbies is she practicing?" Anger burst inside me.

Shooting to my feet, I shouted, "Ya don't know what I've been through! Ya don't know!" My fists were clenched, shaking as tears of rage fell from my cheeks and I began to rant, "I'll teach ya, ya barmy shite! I'll teach ya!" I was clamoring over the edge of the tube, screaming curses when suddenly my head went light and I tumbled to the floor. The world spun sickeningly as Miss Bottoms came to my aid.

"What just happened?" asked a girl.

"Just shut your bloody mouth, alright," Miss Bottoms spat, steadying me by the arm and guiding me back into the tub. "What was all that then?" she asked.

I didn't answer. Rather I lowered myself back into the water and stared ahead, waiting for my head to right itself again.

"No matter," said Miss Bottoms. "Wash the grime out of your hair."

After Miss Bottoms stole a dress from one of the younger girls, a shapely blonde who protested vigorously, she lead me down the halls back the way we had come, heading for The Vexing Valentine. The dress was too large for me, the bosom loose, but I hadn't the mind to care. It was soft and compared to the uniform I had been forced into upon the docks, the dress was simply heavenly. Once I tore my eyes from the ground before me, I was surprised again to see how high the ceiling of this hallway was.

"Ah," said Miss Bottoms when she noticed my gawking. "Do you know why the rooms here are so large?"

"No," I said, realizing that even the walls on either side of us did not rise to the ceiling. They were nothing more than ornamental dividers.

"It takes a little getting used to," she said. "The building is such a strange structure because originally it was nothing more than a series of abandoned warehouses. The Missus was the one who had the vision for something more. She connected them, built rooms, and even turned the one we're headed to now into a night club, The Vexing Valentine. It was just meant to be a front for laundering, that sort of thing, but I suppose we did something right because it actually became quite successful."

"What's a night club?" I ventured.

"Really?" she asked. "Oh, deary, you've got a lot to learn."

Before long we reached the door to The Vexing Valentine. Miss Bottoms halted and looked me over.

"You ready?" she asked me.

I didn't know what I was: lost, terrified, angry. The past few days had been a whirlwind of events spiraling out of control and even now as I stood more comfortably than I had in days, I was bewildered. I hadn't chosen to come here, I'd been freezing on the streets, destined to die when Miss Bottoms found me and started asking questions.

As Miss Bottoms adjusted my dress, trying to compensate for the empty space, a nervous question tugged at me. "Have you ever killed anybody, Miss Bottoms?"

My eyes were shifting between the floor and my new clothes which hung awkwardly. When I dared to peak a glance, she greeted me with a funny sort of smile. After a moment she shook her head and replied, "Haven't we all, dear? Alright, you're as ready as ever. In you get."

Entering The Vexing Valentine for the first time felt like walking through a door leading to yet another strange new world. The vast open room hummed with a hive of activity, greeting me with equally strange, frightening, wondrous, and sinful sights in every direction. The Vexing Valentine was more than just a bar with merry drunken patrons leaning on each other, more than just a cabaret with provocative dancers entertaining an ogling crowd. It was more even than just a gambling ring where fortunes were lost and won. The Vexing Valentine was all of this, yet was somehow imbued with its own powerful mystique.

"So this is a night club," I said as I turned to find Miss Bottoms but she had gone. Had I been so wrapped up in the atmosphere that I had missed her directions? Anxiously, I maneuvered past groups of men puffing cigars, women sipping drinks, and waiters ducking through the crowds. The patrons were dressed peculiarly, at least to my eyes. Most of the men wore the skin of an animal draped over their shoulders or sewn upon their clothing — predatory mammals, serpents, and other industrious beasts. The women wore deceased creatures also but as accessories such as hats adorned with protruding birds — both birds of prey and quainter foraging birds — scarves made from the pelts of foxes, and other creatures equally glamorous and rare.

But in this crowd, I couldn't find The Missus, so I waited alone in The Vexing Valentine with naught but my fears and thoughts.

Da had explained Victainia to me, this country I had so violently entered, and had especially described Sundale, the city I now inhabited and the port city wherein he was raised. He had called it a wondrous yet vile place, at times grand and filled to the brim with excess; at other times brutal and unforgiving. As I watched the women dancing with their wide grins and seductive winks, I couldn't help but watch in awe.

"Miss Over?" a young boy of perhaps twelve looked up at me with folded arms and a tattered vest.

"Yes?" I said taken aback. Looking about me, I saw other young boys like this one peppering the crowd.

"The Mussus wants ya. She's waiting. Don't nobody leaves her waiting, so get ta steppin'."

"Where is she?" I asked and glanced round the crowded floor.

He lifted a finger toward the second floor walkway which wrapped all around the room, the railing crowded with leaning smokers and drinkers. "Up the stairs," he said, "frew the door with the Biggon front of it."

"Biggon?" I asked.

"Yeah, she's the big one," he rolled his eyes and disappeared back into the crowd.

I walked up the stairs and approached the door where the 'big one', a woman more muscular than I had ever seen before, stood guard. "Your name?" she asked.

"Over," I hesitated. "Yevylin Over."

"The newest urchin?" she smiled. "You're more prissy than I was expecting. I expected filthy by the sounds of things. A little disappointed actually. I'm Biggon, and I'll either be the one who beat's you senseless or congratulates you first."

"Oh," I said taken aback.

As she opened the door, she whispered, "I'm hoping for the first. I've had a bad day."

I entered. The air felt thick as I walked forward, toward The Missus who sat upon a massive ornate pillow behind the squat table.

The walk across the room felt like I was wading through a swamp, such was my apprehension. But pushing me onward was something more powerful, a fear of being thrown back to the unforgiving Victanian streets — a sentence that would surely kill me — so harsh had been my treatment thus far. The conditions of how I would die were still uncertain; starvation, freezing, captivity, assault? A foreign affairs constable would string me up, more likely than not. Whatever the cause, another day or two on my own would spell my death, there was no mistaking that.

I walked through the dimly lit room, swimming through the heavy air toward her. The Missus seemed more than a woman. She was a force which I could feel as much as I could see. She watched me enter with her studying eyes, but she did not say a word.

"Sit," she said when my feet finally carried me to the table. There was not a seat in the room, naught but ornate pillows in mounds on either side of the short table.

"Here?" I asked nervously before one such mound of pillows.

"As good a place as any," she said. "Your first time in The Vexing Valentine, I presume?"

"Yes," I said, watching as she raised a pipe to her lips and elegantly puffed.

"Mmm," she nodded. "I can't imagine a first time in this place, not anymore. This building was nothing more than a warehouse when I first saw it. Nothing was here but a big, cold, and empty room. I was younger then, but I suppose that goes without saying. I brought together a group of girls like me and we began to transform it into something more than an abandoned space. Somewhere along the way, I began to learn a few lessons. One of those lessons was to choose wisely those I took under my wing."

Bringing the pipe to her lips, she produced a cloud of smoke that framed her face in a swirling haze. "So," she said, leveling her eyes on me, "you killed a man. I want to hear about it; the whole story from the very beginning." As she spoke she produced a tall glass with a thick stem and placed upon the rim of the glass a wide knife and upon that a small sugar cube. I watched intently as she worked. She poured liquor over the sugar from a dark bottle with glimmers of the deepest green. Then she put a candle to the cube and set the thing afire. The flames flickered as she moved the glass toward me.

"Blow it out," her voice soft, "quickly does it."

I obeyed and extinguished the flame.

"Drop in the sugar and stir."

"What is it?" I asked.

"Not very polite to ask," she smiled. "It's absinthe. It will do you well. Puts hair on the chest, so they say. So, tell me all about it. I want to hear your story."

I nodded and nervously sipped from the glass, coughing at the strength of the drink. "Well," I stammered attempting to collect myself, "I arrived in this country, and first thing I know, I'm robbed blind and imprisoned by a right bastard of a man. I s'pose that's where this story started. I—" I paused. I was jumping into my story, and somehow that didn't feel right, I had learned that much from Da. If I was to tell it, I was to tell it proper and from the beginning. "Damn it," I cursed, then drank my glass dry. "I need another. I flummoxed the damn thing up already. Me Da, he's the storyteller. The story starts with him anyhow, not them damn docks! I'll get to that in a mo'. I hope ya don't mind if I start at the beginning?"

"Be my guest," she raised an inquisitive eyebrow as she passed the bottle my way. Without bothering with all the mixing gullyfluff, I poured myself a second glass, took a sip, and then delved straight into my story.

CHAPTER 3

Not so long ago, me Da, lying upon his deathbed, told me about a bottle of gin. As me Da tells it, it doesn't matter who ya are. Nuns and beggars, generals and thieves, they all prize the drink called Extra Special Reserve Putrid Gin as a drink above all others. But I'm getting ahead of meself.

Me Da was popular in our village on account of his stories. They called him Al Over, a funny name, I know. No one in the village ever knew his real name; I hardly knew it meself. They called him Al Over because when he first came ta town he trotted straight inta the pub. As a new face in town, people were naturally curious. So they asked him, "Where do ya come from?"

"Me?" asked me Da. "I come from all over."

"All over?" asked they. "What kind of answer is that? No one comes from all over. Where're ya from originally?"

Me Da looked inta his beer and smiled. "All over," he replied. He came from Victania originally, ya'll be happy ta hear — from Sundale in fact, but that is not a place people like ta be tied ta where I am from.

So when they asked, "Are ye from the main land, then?" Da said, "Yes, in a manner of speaking."

"In a manner of speaking?" asked they. "So was ye born in the isles then and matriculated inta the main land?"

"Not exactly," said he, "But it wouldn't be far from the truth."

"Maritime past?" asked they.

"Ya ain't lyin'," answered he.

"Navy, private, or pirate?"

"Give it up boys," answered he, "I've done it all."

"Well then," said they, "Perhaps ye can enlighten us."

So me Da told his story of how he traveled about the world. In each region he had enough stories ta fill a book. By the time he had finished his third beer, they had gathered round him, huddled in close ta listen ta his tales. By the end of the night they asked him, "So, are ye setting up kip or is this just another stop on yur travels round the globe?"

"Me traveling days are behind me now, boys. I've got a little girl, and she with no Mum, so I'm settin' up kip. This seems a good spot. We've bid on the empty lot at the end of the lane. Fixin' ta build a house right quick."

"And what can we call ye then?" asked they. But before he could answer, the old drunk in the corner shouted, "'aven't ye been listnin', boys? 'is name's Al! Al Over."

"Shut yur bone box, McKennen," shouted they.

"No, he's quite right," said me Da with a twinkle in his eye. "Al's me name. Al Over."

Thus it came ta be that he was known in those parts forever as Al Over. Me Da worked like the others but he told stories in the pub too. Every night he had another story ta share and the more he told the more they loved him. Soon his name turned ta Mr. Al Over and eventually, jokingly, ta Sir Al Over. He liked that. He rode it out, told newcomers that he was a knight tried and true. Though the patrons knew it wasn't so, they backed him up every time.

When he told a story, he'd use such a powerful voice unlike anyone had ever heard — a real showman. He started by lowering his voice ta a deep baritone then carried it on with gusto. His voice could shake the walls if he willed it.

Me Da, one day he grew ill. It was painful ta see such a great man made so humble by a thing like dying.

Because I loved him I stayed with him. I didn't go a courting like the other girls, didn't have the patience for it anyhow. Some of the boys in the village, they began ta call me an old maid, so in the night I would sneak out ta see the trouble I could cause them lily livered bastards. It was daft things mostly, like leaving garments about their home in hopes the lady of the house would find them and begin asking awkward questions. It made me heart sing when those pansy boys got a whipping.

So there I was at twenty-four years of age, not married, no prospects, no wealth, no dowry, only a wee cottage and a dying Da full of stories and me with a habit of leaving knickers about boys rooms ta get them inta trouble. But that was fine, anything for me Da.

"There ya are," he said one morning as I sat next ta his bed and took up his hand. "There's me gal. Look atcha. Just look atcha. So very beautiful. It does me old heart proud ta see such a lovely face in the family."

"Like Mum?" I asked as I oft had in the past but he only responded by tapping his nose with a wink. I had only ever imagined her, me mum, she having died in childbirth. When I was young, I cried for weeks asking me Mum for forgiveness for killing her. But as I grew older I developed a shadow of her in me mind. A shadow because, for all me Da's stories, there were never any in which she appeared.

"If today's me last day," said he that morning, "I

just want ta look at yur pretty face one last time."

"Don'cha talk like that Da," said I. "It ain't yur time ta go, not yet. Yur sure ta mend soon 'nough."

"No," said he. "No. I can feel it Yevylin. Me soul, it's waiting in line. Can't shove off until them blokes before me get their sins read off. I've got some evil bastards up front, so I'll be round a little while. Even so, I feel can it.

"But, me girl, that's not what I want ta talk about today," said he, his voice tired. "I have a little time left on this earth and I aim ta enjoy it whilst I still can. Ta that end, I have a request of ya. Something ta do for yur old Da afore he dies. If ya hurry ya just might have time ta beat the Reaper. Do ya think ya could do something for me afore I go?"

"'Course Da," said I. "'Course I would."

"There's me gal," said he with a smile. "Most Da's in the world wouldn't think of asking their girls to do something like this but I ain't most and it's important. If ye were a boy, this would prove you were a man. It's a difficult thing I'll ask, but for a woman like you it may prove especially hard, I imagine. Not because yur incapable, so don't be giving me that look. This is what I aim to give ya: passage inta womanhood. And not 'cause of any froo froo marriage. Ya'll be a woman of yur own right, I wager, and that's more than most. Yur strong and smart as a whip so I have faith in ya ta do what I'm asking."

"Course I can, Da," said I anxiously, without a thought as ta what the task could be. "Tell me what it is."

"That's good," said he. His eyes tired, he had trouble lifting his head ta look at me so I put me hand on his chest and tried ta smile. Truth was, I was really quite nervous.

"Have I ever told ya about the Putrid Corpse?" he asked.

"No, Da." I curled me lip in disgust. "I ain't digging up a corpse, if that's wha'cha askin'."

"Do ya really think I'd ask that of ya?"

I shrugged. "It wouldn't be far off."

He smiled weakly at me reaction. "No, Yevylin. It's the place where they make a drink. A very special sort of drink, a kind of gin made in a country ta the east, over in Victania; in the city of Sundale where I grew up. Oh, and it is marvelous. It comes in a black bottle without so much as a label but ya can tell it's from the Putrid Corpse by the cork. Upon it is burned an image of a dead man's face with X's through the eyes and his tongue sticking out." He stuck out his tongue and mimed the face.

"That is vile," said I with a spellbound smile, slapping his arm as he laughed.

"It is," he laughed. "It is, it is! A vile image and a vile name, and it comes from a vile place. But Yevylin, let me tell ya about the flavor. God created the Earth in six days and on the seventh day he rested. Do ya know what he did on that seventh day while he rested, Yevylin? He poured himself a glass of liquor so powerful and so pure that it reminded him exactly of the world he created. The liquor, it reminded him of the waterfalls, of the sounds they make and mist they splash up. The liquor, it reminded him of the sea and the storms which make it rage. It reminded him of the mountains and the sky above them and the place in the middle where they meet. It was as perfect as a liquor can ever be crafted.

"Many years have passed since that day, Yevylin," he sighed. "And through those years man has tried ta distill a drink as powerful and as pure as the one God himself drank the day after creation. They've tried with potatoes and grapes and grains of all sorts. Many a good drink has been made. There have been vodkas, whiskeys, and wines that open yur eyes and caress yur tongue. But they all fall dastardly short. All except one, the Extra Special Reserve Putrid Gin.

"Now," he continued. "This drink is made by a group of the most gleefully vicious of men. They live in a dangerous neighborhood known only as The Gin District, a district named after them own selves, if ya can believe it.

"But before ya trot off on yur errand, I must explain why," he continued. "I have a few stories ta tell. Three stories as luck would have it. I've lived me a long life, Yevylin. A life fraught with trials and tribulations, but three times, joy came in the way of Extra Special Reserve Putrid Gin. If she were a lady, she would be the most sultry and sought after of women, but also the most unattainable. Ya see, Extra Special Reserve Putrid Gin has a few particularities about it. First, it's only available in the pub attached ta the distillery where it's created. Ta remove a bottle from the premises equals death for many men. Thus it is a delicacy which has cost the lives of countless dreamers. Bare that in mind whilst I'm telling me stories."

I paused in my story telling as The Missus filled the void in our conversation with a small chuckle. "You placed your knickers in boys rooms to get them whipped?" She smiled, savoring the idea.

While I told my story, I'd kept my eyes leveled upon the table between us, upon the glowing candlelight and the reflections of it in the bottle. But her response caused me to look up and smile a little despite myself. "A bit."

"A bit clever, a bit mischievous, a bit wicked."

"I've been called worse." My hand shook slightly, and the glass I held shook with it, causing my drink to dribble over the side and spill onto my chin as I attempted to sip. Embarrassed, I placed the glass too hard upon the table causing a clatter.

"I'm sorry," I said bewildered at my own awkwardness. "Ya probably do not care about all this then. It's just, I feel like the reasons are important, the reasons for everything need some explaining. And the reasons come from the stories. But the stories… I can skip them if ya want."

"No," she shook her head then sipped gently on her glass. "I want to hear it all. I want to get the complete image of Miss Yevylin Over. Go on, then."

I nodded and collected my thoughts. "Me Da had a particular way of telling these stories. It don't feel right ta tell 'em any different. I ain't as good, but I'll try. So here's what he told me that day, layin' still and weak on the bed, pausing ta cough or ta catch his breath from time ta time."

CHAPTER 4

It was long ago, Yevelyn, when I was eighteen and finally a man. As me first manly act I decided ta take up a position in the Navy. And why not for a young lad such as meself? A chance ta earn a living, ta travel the world, ta become a war hero.

I was ta ship out on board the VRS Jessimine, a small gun boat on a course ta the colonies down in Africa. Other than this, I had no knowledge of the purpose of our journey. I did not know about the sugar cane uprisings nor about the vicious local bandits and piracy; forced inta the life after being driven from their lands. And I certainly did not know of the disease that was spreading through the colonies like a tidal wave of desperation and despair.

Had I been aware, I cannot say whether I would have made a different choice. I was young and as such I was stupid. This was back when I blindly believed in me country. But seeing the wide world has a way of casting a nasty look about the country of Victania.

I had progressed through me learnin' and passed on proud as any student can be, eyes a twinkle for me future. Joining the Navy would be me first step ta greatness, I was sure of it — as sure as a man can be of anything. So when I told me family that I was ta be joining the Navy, me Ma took it upon herself ta throw me a magnificent party.

Ya never met yur Grandma, Yevelyn, so ya don't know the socialite she was. She delighted in company, more so than any other woman I ever met. A socialite for the ages, such an entertainer was she, even the upper class would give her an allowance of time and company despite our existence on the fringe of their high society world. Do ya know why they did this? Because of her parties.

"The thing to bear in mind when entertaining the guests," she said of parties, the imitation head of a kestrel upon her hat. "We do not invite just a few of the ladies in high standing; instead we fuel a little gossip about them. And to liven things, we invite a controversial guest or two. It's the spice of the party, the flavor. We give the ladies a little tang, a little intrigue by inviting the perfect combinations of guests. A bit of outrage will hook them like a fish, but just a bit."

The name of each potential guest was written

upon a small card, and when me ma found that one guest or another did not fit her recipe for a party, she scoffed and tossed the card inta the fire. It made her eyes glow ta watch it burn.

When I caught her tossing away cards for me party, I asked her, "Why do you throw them in the fire?" In those days me voice mimicked that of the upper class like me parents had taught me.

She looked down at me for a long while before she answered. "For the good of the party, dear."

But that wasn't the truth, Yevelyn. She was an artist. She cut away from the guest list like a sculptor cuts away from the stone ta reveal something breathtaking. It made her feel powerful, the smolder and the smoke, as if she were casting away a breathin' being ta burn, curl, and char inta dust.

Mine was the party for the ages. Ya would have thought a duke was returning from a successful war, but no. It was I who was leaving and she wished me ta be remembered.

Lieutenant Hinde was his name — the man who, during my party, introduced himself ta me hours inta the night by catching me arm while I stood in a boring crowd of prestigious ladies talking ta me of me future. "Excuse us," he said ta them with a short nod, "but I'll be stealing the young sir away for a while. Give him some pointers about the Navy, that sort of thing. You'll join me, young lad, won't you?"

I nodded vigorously, relieved for the excuse ta abandon the crowd, but nervous of what direction our conversation would take. But me nervousness shifted ta anxious curiosity as he led me out the door ta the damp streets shining with the aura of gas lamps. What could he tell me that was so secret a thing that he led me out and inta the night? I hadn't the foggiest notion.

"The man of the hour," he said smacking me back with a little ta much force for a sober man. "And a Navy man, too. I like that." Pausing a moment, he studied me before smiling a wicked smile. "I've brought you something, a gift rare and dangerous but choice, young sir. Have you heard of Extra Special Reserve Putrid Gin?"

"No," said I, intrigued.

"What about the pub, The Putrid Corpes?"

I shook me head.

"Hm," he said a little disappointed. "I suppose you're a bit young. Once you make it into the wide world, you'll hear tales of it time and again, make no mistake, squire. You'll meet scurvy bastards claiming to have found a bottle but it never turns out to be the real thing. I've tasted it from the source, you see, and once you've had a sip, that taste will be etched into your memory deeper than any other thing. You'll know a false bottle when you taste it. Oh, it might be grand but never quite the same.

"The real thing," he continued, "rarely leaves Sundale without a hand or two dying over its extrication. Liquid gold some call it. Well, two weeks back I found myself sniffing where my nose didn't rightly belong, and wouldn't you know, I was lucky enough to find me a bottle of the stuff. Paid a pretty penny for it too. Thought it'd make a good gift. How does the sound of that strike you?"

"Grand," said I.

"Grand," he smiled. "You'd be a fool or a coward to deny an offer like this. Most will never get an opportunity like it. Tell you what: go find a mate who can hold his liquor. If word catches your ship that you've tasted Putrid Corpse, you'll have a reputation all right."

Running in and out as quickly as the increasingly gay party would allow, I grabbed me mate Johnny and the three of us met outside. It was a dank, cold, and biting night, so Johnny and I shivered as we stood alongside this strange gentleman.

The Lieutenant looked over his shoulder and peered round each corner before producing the blackest of black bottles. "It should be said," he uncorked the bottle with his teeth. "If you're caught with a bottle by the wrong sorts, the results aren't pretty. Stripped, bound by the wrists, often strung up, beaten with canes or blackjacks, feet burned and tongue, eh, smoothed — the top of it shaved so you cannot taste again — that's the punishment the underworld has put on discovery of this bottle. So, boys," his eyes glowed, "thirsty?"

I smiled and nodded. If ever there was a way ta capture a young man's attention, this was it. Me anticipation mounted so high it would have been impossible for the reality of any other drink ta live up ta this story. But so wondrous a drink it was, so strange, flavorful, and dangerous that the myth behind it only enhanced the wonder of Extra Special Reserve Putrid Gin.

He passed me the bottle. "You're the man of the hour. Have the first sip, sir." I did. The smell rushed outward, but unlike the name, it was not putrid, it was intoxicatingly sweet. He nodded as Johnny bounced on his toes with anticipation.

The flavor! Yevelyn, let me tell ya about the flavor. When the rolling sea was first made, before it was populated with fish and fowl, it was a pure, ever flowing thing. God used the Earth like a great mug of tea and pressed the sea ta his lips and drew in a deep swallow, and so sweet and refreshing was it that he took the recipe and hid it within his almighty pocket ta be revealed only ta a chosen few at the right time. As the good book says, those who are low shall be made high, and it shall be done with Extra Special Reserve Putrid Gin.

CHAPTER 5

Upon entering the Navy and setting out ta sea, the tale of me brush with the bottle of Extra Special Reserve Putrid Gin did much ta elevate me within the minds of me peers. Long days of labor were often made easier through the telling of stories; each of us with our favorite tales of conquest, failure, and triumph. But me life had not been as adventurous as me fellow sailors, so when it came time for me ta tell a tale, I had nothing ta speak of. After a little goading, I reluctantly told the story Lieutenant Hinde had told me and then, in a rather off-hand sort of manner, I mentioned I had tasted the drink.

The boys were aghast. "Did they come after ye, the Putrid Corpse thugs?" one of the boys asked. "I heard tell, they track any bloke who's had a hand at removin' a bottle from the pub. Cut out yur tongue, that's what they say. So, how did ye escape them?"

Taken off guard that these boys not only knew of the drink but they knew the lore behind it ta, I did me best ta build me reputation just as Lieutenant Hinde had suggested. "That is true," said I. "But for the details. They donna cut it out. They shave it, skin 'n' sear the top clean off with a red hot knife. Surely they were after me from that day forward but I skipped town, boys, joined the Navy. But we must be careful; they have agents 'round the world seeking out stolen bottles. Understand boys? We keep this amongst ourselves."

Anxiously I waited for the rumors ta spread and of course they did. Soon I found meself facing awed young men asking for me ta share the tale. Whilst me story was mayhap rooted in truth, with each telling, the tale grew more unruly and fantastic. I soon found meself claiming that The Putrid Corpse pub kept a hunchback chained in the back, viciously surveying the patrons, eager ta spill blood with its calloused, deformed fists like knotty clubs. Keeping watch of the door, he'd cry, "*Thieves!* Under order of the Corpse, I smasheth thee!" And then he indeed smashethed them.

Me career in the Navy was filled with ever more fantastic stories. I witnessed and participated in many a great and terrible thing; as life became hellish me stories took on a grander scale. Me life became a nightmare and the stories somehow carried me through it. I burned villages, watched them take light and breed dancing flames which licked the skin of natives. I had joined the navy a young and naive boy but then I learned the smell of burning flesh, witnessed shards of wood fly through the air, disemboweled men groaning, kneeling men pleading, and oddly calm men firing their last shots. I could never have remained the same boy who was celebrated at that party four years earlier.

Then one day it was over. Me four years were up. I would have no more of the military.

I returned home ta discover the world had changed. Something happened and now me Ma was more or less ignored by the people she had called friends four years previous. It was as though she was on the cusp of drowning and shortly after I returned she lost the will ta tread water.

Instead of a party upon me return, me drunken Da slapped me shoulder and said, "You're a man now, son. I have a secret for ya. Want ta know what it is?"

I watched him, his head rocking a little ta the drunken sway, but I didn't answer.

"The world is a shite place. Remember that. Everything ya do, it's amounting to a better view on a pile of shite. And if ya stop tryin' — well then it all just washes over ya, holds ya down, suffocates ya, and then one day ya die." He smiled an uncharacteristically charming grin.

I tried ta ignore his words and focus on anything else but what I saw were the empty bookshelves. "Where have all the books gone Da?" I asked.

He laughed heartily in the way only a drunk without hope can. "Burned them last winter ta keep warm."

CHAPTER 6

Three days I was home before I left walking and never turned back round. Me feet carried me back ta the docks. Without direction or a plan, I found employment on a merchant ship and escaped ta ride the sea ta the east, ta India. It was there, in India of all the places in the world, me life dipped ta its lowest point. It was also there where I found a second drink of Extra Special Reserve Putrid Gin.

Me mind was in a terrible state. I fell ta despairing, submerged by the weight of overwhelming guilt for the things I'd done in the navy, for the state of me troubled family, and for leaving them far behind without so much as a goodbye. Surely this had earned me a damning.

Upon arriving in India, I immediately abandoned me vessel and found meself staggering through a foreign and unfamiliar land. The people were dark, the smells intense, and the sounds strange and entrancing. The bright colors the people wore contrasted the heavy earth tones of the streets. Seas of faces swarmed about me everywhere I turned. The crowds pushed me deep inta the city while the music of their rolling language babbled like an ever present brook.

Within this pained stupor, I somehow found me way inta an opium den. The money I had was quickly spent and me body numbed ta its very core. If I have any regret in life, it was not turning away at that moment. In the opium dens, me despair burrowed through me numbed soul, deep inta me bones. In time, me body withered; a soft shell filled with the pieces of a human and nothing more.

Months passed me by as I rotted away in the dens, spending the last of me coin. Me head in a fog, me stomach empty of food, I found meself abandoned on an empty street with nothing but the Untouchables ta keep me company. The Untouchables — a people whose very existence is a crime. They are not accepted inta society but are outcast ta lives of suffering and desolation on the streets. These shivering, malnourished, often dying people were me friends, if ya can call them that. Lepers with their skin slipping from their bones in disgusting displays, the malformed with great growths and missing extremities, they endured a pitiful existence. And the dying, oh the dying. The dying lay on the street corners festering with maggots, hardly able ta speak above a breath as they were eaten alive. It was they who took pity on me and would speak ta me in a tongue I could not understand. And when they died, as they often did, it was I who cried for them and no one else.

When ya are one with the Untouchables, ya are destined for an early death. So it was only a small matter of time before something wretched took hold within me and I fell horribly ill. For days I lay by the wayside while me bowels churned in such agony. Forget crawling, Yevelyn, forget reasoning and speech. I was nothing but pain and dread.

Then she came.

From time ta time, Sister Rosetta passed through these streets with a heartbroken look about her. This day her beautiful, sorrowful eyes scanned us, covering her mouth as she fought back tears. Ta some she bent over and offered them a gentle touch. She whispered in their ears or held them close even though their rotting flesh brushed against her habit as she waved over other nuns ta place these poor people upon gurneys ta be carried away.

On this day she did just like she always did, tears and all, and she did it for me. Her hand was rough rather than soft like I had imagined but even so it felt sweet against me arm as she gently held me. "Sir," she asked and when I looked on her I saw a young face. "What's your name?"

I tried ta speak but only a hoarse breath escaped me lips.

Tears rolled down her cheeks, sweat beaded on her brow, and she spoke in a wavering voice, "Could I... offer you a bed for the night? Food?"

I blinked against the dust in me eyes and tried ta nod.

CHAPTER 7

"How does it feel?" I asked her weakly as she fed me stew. The fact that she spoke Victanian was a miracle.

"This?" she asked in her thick accent which I didn't have the mind ta place.

I nodded.

"It is hard, but good, no? It is good to know I am easing a little pain. It is why I'm here in India: to lend some comfort. God called me to this place and I obeyed." Even as she spoke I could see her holding back a portion of the truth. I could see it in the way her eyes were always red from crying.

Days passed slow. Me few memories were of pain, interrupted on occasion by the beautiful nun, Rosetta. I mended a little at a time. Then I began ta notice the men lying on either side of me, each upon his own thin blanket with eyes sunken and lips pulled tight as they rasped in air. Was I like them? Of course I was, just another refugee in the home for dying souls.

One morning I opened me eyes and the rasping had stopped. The man ta me right had quit his spasms, his life departed. I winced as I watched the nuns brush the flies away from his eyes but I did not cry for him as they carried him away. Me heart had been whittled down over the years. Empathy had departed.

"How do ya handle it, seeing those ya care for die?" I asked that afternoon as Rosetta fed me a curry of potatoes and pungent spice.

"I don't." she struggled for words, lips quivering. "I handle it terribly. It is difficult in two ways. Either I find myself growing fond of them and for them I cry or I take refuge in the knowledge that they are dying and look on them not as humans but as objects. And for that I am truly beset by sorrow." She had paused in her task of feeding me and I watched her carefully. "I try to take comfort in knowing that their suffering has passed and that perhaps their spirits are in a place more kind. But there are times when I am able to help someone, to nurse them back into health. For those moments I'm joyous."

Months passed before I was returned ta health enough ta leave, yet I found meself indebted ta Rosetta, though she never claimed it. But more than this, I didn't want ta leave her. I stayed and worked scrubbing festering sores, cleaning the foul leavings of the bed ridden, and listening ta those who would speak even if I could not understand their rolling language.

I never became a righteous or devout man. I clung ta the young nuns company like a leech clinging ta yur leg. I needed sustenance for me wretched soul. And I found meself growing fond of her.

In working with the dying, every day was a terrible struggle. By simply sitting next ta some of these untouchables, I was forced ta wrestle with me bowels, ta hold in me stomach, and contain meself. When cleaning sores and pulling maggots, I thought I would die of disgust. I thought I would catch some foul disease that would end me.

But more than this — more than the physical nature of the work — seeing these people in utter anguish every day, I could not bear it like Rosetta could. I descended inta fits of panic and hid meself away in quiet corners for hours at a time. And when I was diligent, I broke inta sobs as I worked for hours and hours and hours. Helping the dying proved far more taxing on me soul than burning the living.

"Sister Rosetta," said I one day. "I can take this no longer! I am trying but I can't go out there any more ta watch them suffer meaninglessly and then ta—ta just die. Where is the meaning in this? Where is God in this?" Tears streamed down me face in shame and agony.

Her eyes lingered on mine for a still moment. "I had hoped…" she trailed off. Blinking away tears, she turned away from me ta dry her eyes on her habit. "I am sorry," her voice shook. "I am familiar with how you feel. It is difficult. There is no great meaning in their suffering. And perhaps there is no meaning in our easing their passing. Without us they would die all the same. But an act of compassion, even to the hopeless and dying, is a worthwhile thing. Isn't it?"

"I…" I couldn't meet her eyes. "I can't. Not anymore. I tried. I tried desperately ta be with you, but I…"

"You're a good friend," she said kindly. "Come, it's time for us to prepare for your leaving."

I followed her up crooked stairs and through an open doorway. Upon an uneven wooden stool she bade me sit, then from a cupboard she pulled a black bottle. "I have a confession for you," she said. "I'll miss you when you're gone. And another confession: I have a small weakness for drink. For medicinal purposes, you understand." She gave me a mischievous smile. "It is my secret. I've never bought a bottle but they have a way of finding their way to me. And this bottle is my favorite. Two years ago a strange man gifted me this bottle of gin, a man I hadn't met before nor seen since. I've been savoring it. It is called The Extra Special Reserve Putrid Gin

— a fitting name for this place, if you will excuse a laugh on such a dark topic. Sit down. You will enjoy it I think."

CHAPTER 8

I looked back on the monastery only once as I walked along the dirty street.

I left India as soon as I was able and took up crew on *The Esmeralda*. Though I did me best ta avoid me home over the years that followed, there's little choice in the matter when ya are a sailor. Eventually, trade routes took me home ta Sundale. I worked the days on the great harbor Sundale is famous for but during the nights I took ta roaming the streets.

The damp cobbled roads reflected patterned arrangements of the yellow gas lamps and as I walked, I kept the reflections at the edge of me vision, letting them twist and morph around outlines of square stones in strange, dancing ways.

Two forces guided me along the twisting Sundale streets as I walked in the night. The first was a pressure pushing outward from the neighborhood

51

where I used ta live. I found meself with a pang in me heart veering in sharp turns where the roads grew familiar. The second force was patient and imperceptible, an ethereal thread connecting me heart ta home. As I wandered night after night, it waited for me mind ta slip inta a deep sort of thought, and then guided me feet back in home's direction.

I was taken by surprise when I found meself standing before me old home in the dead of night. Wearily, I watched it — me home — standing before those darkened windows unsure of whether I would approach or turn away. As night passed, I migrated ta a near-by bench and as the dew settled and morning came, I was pulled from me thoughts when the door ta me parents house opened.

It was a face I did not recognize. A young and wealthy looking man emerged wearing the skin of a fox stitched ta the sleeve of his jacket. Quickly I rose, leveling accusing eyes on him as I approached. He gripped his cane tightly and shouted, "You there, halt! What mean you of assailing yourself on me so gruffly?"

"Assailing?" I asked confused. "No, I'm looking for me family. They live in that house."

"My house?" He was astonished and insulted at the thought. "You're gravely mistaken."

"No," I shook me head and pointed. "That one there. That's me family's."

"That one there?" he scoffed. "In point of fact, that house belongs to me and has for some time. Now please, this is a nice neighborhood. Be on your way before I'm forced to call a constable."

"How did ya come by it then?" I asked desperately. "Who did ya purchase it from?"

"The Royal Victanian Bank," answered the man. "Now I've been patient with you. Why don't you come over here, I want to show you something. See there, just down there at the end of the way." He pointed to a small, round building with over-sized windows. "That's a lucky new addition the home owners have banded together to put up. Within is a nice young man with a billy club, and this here," he pulled a small metal whistle from his pocket. "This is the alarm. Thirty seconds and he'll begin educating you with the blunt side of a thick rod."

He placed the whistle ta his lips and raised an eyebrow. He blew a long, shrill note.

I ran.

In the coming days, I learned little of me family. Were they destitute? Holed away in a ghetto? Or had something else happened ta them? Perhaps they were back on their feet in some city on the other side of Victania. The bank was of little help, serving ta only build me frustration. Seeking out me mother's friends was also fruitless. There was nothing ta be done but ta remain ignorant. I had been alone before but somehow now, without family in the world, I was more alone and helpless than I had ever felt previous. I never learned if me family was still of this world.

Except for ya, Yevelyn. And how one thing leads ta another just happens ta involve me last bottle of Extra Special Reserve Putrid Gin.

CHAPTER 9

Angry at the world — that's what I became. A vicious heat roared within me seeking violence, seeking someone ta revenge me troubles upon. The ever present need ta lash out, ta destroy something or ta hurt someone, was always there.

From a drunken stew of frustration and hatred a singularly dangerous quest was born — a task through which I could seek some sort of redemption. I would gain a bottle of Extra Special Reserve Putrid Gin for meself. What for? Just ta prove I could or ta receive the punishment I deserved for abandoning me family. Or maybe I just wanted ta break something.

That night electricity crackled within me spine as I fixated on the stories of that notorious pub, The Putrid Corpse. Some of the stories were told ta me, some of them thought up by me, and I no longer knew the difference. I walked into the dark streets leaving the comfort of the gas lamps behind me. As I searched the winding ways towards The Gin District, the air grew more fowl and the rats more plentiful. So ta were the stumbling drunks, pursed lipped whores, and young hoodlums who eyed me with a predatory stare. I passed them with nary a thought.

Before The Putrid Corpse even came inta sight, I could hear the rambunctious sounds of the echoed voices from within. I walked steadily onward. Then a sound, a cough and a curse, issued behind me. Peering over me shoulder, two figures cloaked by night walked at a distance behind me. As I pressed on they drew ever closer. Me skin grew agitated as if it were swarming with ants. When I sped me pace ta a trot, me pursuers did likewise.

Rounding the corner, the lights from the windows of The Putrid Corpse came inta view and I hurried towards it, hailing two men who leaned against the windows, each wearing top hats featuring skins of once great reptiles. They ignored me and showed only a mild interest, one nudging the other, as me pursuers came inta view.

"Could ya lend me a hand, gentlemen?" I asked as I planted me feet before the pub and turned ta face me pursuers.

"Why?" came their bored reply.

Bewildered by his nonchalance, I turned back ta

the man with a confused look. Halfheartedly he smiled. "Ain't me problem. B'sides, why ruin a bit o' fun?"

"Oi gents," one of me pursuers shouted, forehead, nose and cheeks lit by the dim light of the pub, eyes and mouth in shadow. "This ain't got nofin ta do wif ya fine lot. Just gonna nick his pocketbook is awl. Do'ya mind?"

"He's got no colors," said one of the men behind me. "We've got nofin' ta do wif this."

"Fanks." His voice was younger than I suspected and as he neared his features came ta match but in the dim light I could see the knife in his hands. As he neared, and as the smaller of the two cut off me path for escape, he fingered the tip of his knife as if placating it for lack of blood. "Oi, bloke," he motioned ta me with the knife. "Ya know how this goes, don'cha? Empty them pockets right quick an' I don't gut'cha. Quickly does it, I'm in a hurry."

Empty me pockets? I had been seeking violence and it had found me. The terrible furnace of shame and regret billowed inta a dark anger. I relished the opportunity for him ta near, come knife blade or bruised knuckles. The lad approached, for he was truly a lad now that I could fully behold him. His comrade flanked me while he kept his distance. As I lowered me hand inta me jacket pocket the lad nodded and said, "That's right. Nofin' funny now."

The twinge in his voice betrayed his lack of confidence.

I watched his feet as he moved in closer and adjusted me stance ever so slightly. As the ground between us lessened I tensed for just a moment. It had been years since I had fought and for a fraction of a moment I felt a tinge of pre-emptive regret, the same regret I had felt years earlier in the Navy. But me mind was set and me conviction for violence strong.

Whipping me jacket wide ta me side, I stepped in on the lad and wrapped the knife wielding hand with the fabric of me jacket. With a sudden expression of pure animal survival, the lad thrashed with his caught hand, attempting ta twist his knife inta me flesh. I wrapped me arm 'round his forearm and yanked up. The pressure of the flat side of the blade pressed against me side. In a fit of panic, I pushed the lad away, sending him off in one direction and me off in the opposite.

"Get 'im!" came the shriek of his young accomplice.

Scrambling ta me feet, I lunged for my assaulter who lay upon his back. He twisted ta regain his balance while struggling ta hold his knife steadily outstretched before him. I reached him as he swung his arm, hitting me thigh and as he retracted for the stab, I lifted me leg and plummeted the heel of me boot upon his knee with a wicked force.

He screamed in shock. His body clenched in pain. I kicked the knife from his hand and then rammed me heel on his knee again for good measure.

The lad erupted inta pained cries and clutched his knee. Tears streamed down his face. Not knowing what ta make of the situation, I looked about me and saw the men behind me shaking their heads before they shrugged. The boy at me flank rushed ta us and I turned on him fearing he would attack but he rounded me and cried, "Blimey, ya really hurt 'im, ya bastard!"

I stepped back and watched the scene, scratching me head and feeling a right arse. "Damn it, boy, let me see it," I huffed as I bent over him.

"Ya broke it, ya cock! Broke me knee," he shrieked.

"I didn't break yur bleeding knee, let me see it."

He reached a shaking hand, lifted his pant leg and revealed an awkward joint. The cap of his knee rested off center. "Look what ya made me do," I said as I shook me head. "I was in the navy, ya arse. Don't mug a man unless yur good and ready for it. Well, ya are buggered now. Stupid arse." The boy cried and I looked 'round us again ta see if we had attracted attention. But those who noticed hardly seemed ta care. "Oh, shut up. Well, come on then. Best get ya mended."

I helped the boy ta his feet and wrapped an arm about him as his young accomplice took ta his side. There was not much ta be done about him but find a piece of wood ta use as a splint, wrap up his leg, and send him on his way.

As I watched the two of them limp off, I more or less came ta me senses. Something had shifted and the anger I felt had been snuffed out with a new uncomfortable feeling. The Putrid Corpse could wait another night so I headed back in the way of the docks. Before I had made it ta far I came across an admiral of the red, a man so proper drunk he was falling over himself and laughing all the while. As I passed him he called out ta me, "Ya won't believe it!"

"What?" said I out of impulse.

Stumbling closer, he lifted up a black bottle and smiled wide. "I stole this." He burst inta a fit of laughter. "I stole it an' I'm gonna be ripe with coin! Ha ha!" Me eyes went wide as they beheld the bottle he clutched in his filthy hands. He pressed one blackened finger ta his lips and said, "They never s'pected nofin'."

"I'll buy that from ya," said I quickly. "Thirty notes right here. I've got it here. Just a second."

But as the man babbled he also began tilting and I cocked me head as I watched. As if the world had been slowly pulled out from under him, the man fell ta the ground and began ta snore. I bent over and prodded his chest but was answered only with a loud, rumbling snort. Looking round, I found the street deserted, just the two of us and the dark of night, not a light, not a star, only the distant barking of a stray dog in the far off distance. I bit me lip, snatched the bottle and strode off. But I couldn't leave him with nothing so hurriedly I pulled a handful of notes from me pocketbook, curled them up, and pressed them inta his hand.

CHAPTER 10

I finally had a bottle of me own. But the feeling in me heart whilst I held it in me hands was bittersweet. I placed it upon a shelf and left it there untouched for days. There the bottle sat without purpose and often I found meself watching it. It was as if I was praying, praying for something ta speak ta me. But nothing spoke. Not from the bottle, anyway.

In short order, I found meself again walking through the night, the bottle hidden away unopened in me room. I wandered because nowhere felt like home. I wandered because each step carried me further from regret, at least for a little while. I wandered because mayhap I was hoping ta find something.

When me ship set sail, it left me behind ta wander the Sundale streets, a vagrant whose endless journey was fueled by two years pay in his pocket.

Me walks often led me through Graendamon, a small section of town stowed away behind Portend like a dirty secret. Walk past the markets, past the opera house, past posh pubs, and curiosity shops — and if the streets are getting dirty, the people a bit more down in their luck, yur on the right path. In Graendamon, the theatres make way for cathouses as the muffled sounds of the opera dies. In its place comes the boisterous sounds of burlesque, show tunes, and jeering crowds.

Up and down the way I meandered, pressing through crowds as I walked without a destination. It wasn't the dancers or whores who brought me here, it was the overflowing noise of the street; the nightly bustle as blokes pressing their way inta the smoky theaters. From within could be heard their cries of goading and delight. As I listened ta the sounds of the shows through the brick walls, I found the noise in me head drowned out. Leaning against a wall, I could pause ta smoke me pipe, watch the shuffling mass of people, and relax for a moment.

One night, feeling the worse for drink, I walked ta the end of the way where the crowds thinned inta not more than a hum of faint noise. I leaned against a gas lamp and rubbed away the sickly dizzy feeling caused by a long night of hard drink. The light of the lamp faded away inta darkness and I watched the area between the two; the area where the light fades away like the edge of a spirit.

Then the carriage came. At first I only heard the clopping of hooves and the wheels rolling against cobbled stones. It burst inta the light like a flash of a vision. As it sped by, I caught sight of a wide-eyed man in a top hat watching out of the carriage window as he leaned out and shouted ta the driver, pointing further down the way and motioning him onward. Then darkness overtook them again; the carriage not but the noise of wheels growing further away. By the sound of it, I guessed it had turned at a few blocks down the way.

Strange. I looked round me ta see if others had witnessed this odd sighting, but no. I needed ta walk, ta clear me head, and pursuing the carriage seemed as fine a destination as the next. I hadn't the mind ta catch it, just needed a direction ta follow. So ignoring me head and the rocking world around it, I followed where the sounds of the carriage seemed ta have led. Perhaps a daft thing ta do, Yevylin, but I didn't expect ta find anything; just another stroll inta the night.

I turned inta an alley, shrugging away the prickling feeling on the back of me neck. With the darkness so complete, I sucked hard on me pipe turning the tobacco inta a dim red glow as I groped against the nearest wall. It was not the dank scenery that caused me ta pause, nor was it the smell of garbage, nor the sound of an unseen crow cawing in the night. It was the soft thing me foot touched, wrapped in rough cloth. *It moved.* Me breath caught in me throat, the thing shuddered and whimpered, rose and fell, breathing a desperate sort of breath, moaning just over a whisper, a sound I had once meself moaned: despair.

Me breath grew heavy as the sound of me heart bounded in me ears. I landed hard upon a knee before it, its breath quick with panic. Reaching for it, the sack felt coarse, she — for I could tell by her breath she was a woman — recoiled at me touch. But she could not recoil far. She was damaged with her head covered by a burlap sack. I pulled the sack away.

"No," her voice was a swallowed, pained thing; shallow and hardly understandable. Pushing against the ground, her hands couldn't bear the weight and she fell, limp with pain; terrified.

I fumbled for a match, striking it ta get a better look. It sputtered ta life revealing a face broken and discolored.

"Good God!" I gasped as me eyes welled with tears.

The alley was dark, and when I looked round for help, there was not a soul anywhere nearby. Without a thought ta the contrary, I lifted her broken body and stumbled down the street, fighting the awkward way her body hung in me arms as I screamed for help.

Her voice bubbled and I shushed her like one calms a child. "I've got ya," I whispered in her ear. "I've got ya, don't ya worry."

A couple saw us and pressed themselves against a wall, eyes wide. I pleaded, "She's badly hurt. I need a physician, anything!" The man shook his head frantically and ushered his companion away. Even as I made it back ta Graendamon, the waning crowds watched me warily, parting as I carried her; begging.

The first door I saw I banged open with a shoulder and shouted, "Clear that table if you won't do anything else ya bastards!" The music stopped, the dancers upon the stage craned their necks ta see the spectacle we were.

"Sir, you can't bring her in here."

"If ya turn me away I'll gut ya, damn piss ant!" I heard meself shout but me eyes were all for yur mother who was bruised, broken, and crying silent tears.

"What's happening here?"

"Get someone," I shouted as I spun and found a stately woman behind me. "A physician, a priest, a nun, a barber for bugger sake. Just go get somebody!"

Yur mother spoke. I turned back and covered me mouth, tears falling from me face as I struggled ta know what ta do. Her words came as little more than a choked breath, "Bebe... Bebe."

Wrap me heart in coarse rope, squeeze it tight,

stop me heart from beating, and let me die. Any pains in the world I will suffer not ta see that sight again. Her belly was large: she was pregnant.

CHAPTER 11

"By some miracle, the unborn child is alive," I was told as yur nameless, battered young mother lay clinging ta life upon a wooden bed within a physician's office.

"Will she give birth soon?" I asked. She had fallen inta a fitful sleep and every hour it seemed she was less likely ta wake again.

"Indeed, that may very well be the case, however—"

"However?" I asked in a cold voice.

"The child will be premature. Chances are very high that she'll be a stillbirth. And if the child does make it, taking care of it is going to be very expensive, you understand." He studied me clothes as I sat over yur mother, watching her, stroking her hair as gently as I was able.

"And, what about the mother?" I asked.

"The mother's not likely to last more than a few days and even that is unlikely. She certainly will not survive the birth. Perhaps," the man hesitated. "Perhaps it might serve you better to allow me to bring her to a church where she can die peacefully. They'll pray for her, perhaps save her soul."

I shook me head. "No."

He nodded, a patient sort of condescension in his eye. "I don't think you quite understand—"

"I'll pay for it," I replied.

"I don't mean to pry, but why? You don't know her. You hardly have a connection to her at all. And in all probability your money will go to waste."

"I'll pay for it," I repeated.

"I see. And you understand the costs?"

"Yes," me voice above a whisper. "I've got... something valuable. I just want ya ta do yur best. Take care of her as best ya can, save the child, and I'll return with the money ya need. Ya have me word on that."

"And you're a man of your word, sir?"

"Yes," I hesitated. "I am today."

I sold the bottle of Extra Special Reserve Putrid Gin and the doctor lived up ta his word.

CHAPTER 12

The Missus was perched upon satin pillows that shimmered their ethereal shine under the glow of the lamps. I chanced a peek and she watched me intently, elegant in her focus. The glimmer of the fabric — always in the corner of my vision no matter where I looked — coupled with my exhaustion, the effects of the drink, and the swirling smoke of her pipe made everything around her seem surreal.

I paused in my storytelling, feeling wholly anxious and awkward. Something felt strange about telling my Da's stories — stories that weren't properly mine — especially telling them for the first time. Before the telling, I was so very sure that these stories were necessary, but now that confidence — if it was indeed confidence and not just the ramblings of a confused girl — left me.

When she spoke, I watched the table anxiously. The smoke from the candles, ebbing away their waxy glow, rose and swirled, and the smoke from the pipe in her hands settled as it spread amongst the bottle and the high stemmed glasses casting murky green shadows.

"And, here I was thinking," she said in a soft voice, "that you were such a quiet girl."

I searched for a reply but none came so I bit my lip and waited.

"Ah," she said, "there it is. You're quiet until you're not. Your story — it all comes back around, does it not? You didn't plan on ending the night with being born? As I see it, the circumstances of your birth matter little when compared to the actions you take in life. Unless, of course, those circumstances motivated you to become who you are today, if you will, which at this point I dearly hope they are, for your sake."

"There's more," I said nervously.

"Right. Well then, we are burning the night away."

CHAPTER 13

Though questions about me Mum chewed at me mind, I asked nothing about her. It was clear that there was nothing more ta be said. She had spoken only a few words ta me Da before she died and left him with a child, me, ta care for. After hearing this I felt as though I should be more affected by the news. Me head was flummoxed but I did not cry, and while I had questions, none were particularly coursing with emotion.

"So, Yevylin," me Da said weakly, his hand shaking as he reached for me and I took it up, his palms worked rough over the years. "Before I go," his voice had grown so weary, "there's some things I'd like ta ask of ya. Ya see, our family is gone, me girl, and they've been gone for nearly thirty years. When I die, ya'll be what's left of us. If I die and ya stay in the village, ya'll be living on charity if yur lucky, but ya should never live on charity for long, lest ya be resented for it. And besides, ya deserve better.

"Yevylin," his eye looked about the ceiling as he spoke, as if searching for something lost. "Victania was the country where we were forged. In that country ya were born. Ta keep living here, in this village, ya'd be wasting yurself. I ask ya, if ya feel yur up for it, ta instead go ta Victania, ta me home city of Sundale. Forge yur spirit of steel, find something ta be remembered by, even if it's only a spark of something." Then he simply tapped his nose, saying, "And while yur there, keep an eye open for a bottle of Extra Special Reserve Putrid Gin. Methinks... Mayhap if only a little time has passed, perhaps I'll be living still. Bring it back so I can have one last taste. I would like that, one last taste, the last taste I never had..."

In the coming days he grew very weak. I sat by him and he hardly had the strength ta speak. His eyes watched me with a longing look as if questioning why I'd not yet left him. Then, not much time later, I entered his room and smelled the stink of death. In the doorway I covered me face with a sleeve and watched him for a long while. He lay there stiff, unmoving, cold. Overtaken with a sudden need ta escape the village, ta leave the whole bloody place behind me, I found meself diving inta his room ta snatch his old travel bag. I quickly filled it with anything I could think of: money, clothes, trinkets, odds and ends; even the three little pieces of jewelry me Mum had left ta me when she died. Before I set off, I told the doctor of me Da's death but I didn't follow him back. I took up me things and ran.

Me head was like stormy weather, like clouds on either side coming together, thunder clapping where they meet. The clouds were uncertainty, the thunder anger, and the winds the hidden desire I had had long before this day — ta escape the village once and for all. I'd always had the desire ta run away ta Victania but never the motivation. The motivation was thick as soup now.

I took ta the sea upon a passenger ship I can't remember the name of (Da could always remember the names), and as the days passed long and slow, me thoughts of anger and uncertainty shifted ta curiosity as I began ta think of the stories I'd heard about the country of Victania. In me mind were cloudy images of amazing cities, gritty and thick with people who always bustled on important errands I couldn't fathom the reasons for.

I dreamed of the inventions. I'd heard of the apothecaries and their witches' brews of expensive elixirs all said ta be the devil's work, providing unnatural remedies or devious afflictions ta whoever consumed them. And of machines, not more than a few poor illustrations of trains had I seen; long machines that travel distances along metal paths. I could imagine the sound, a whirring noise mayhap and smelling like a sweet scented fire.

Rumors came ta our village a year or two previous of an even more modern invention: the boiler-carriage. Imagine it: the power of a train engine now upon the very streets of Victania, led without beast, led only by the power of mans ingenuity.

While on the ship, I felt the salty sea air on me face for the first time, felt it waft up me nose proper like. Me Da used ta talk about the sea air like it was something magical, something ta guide young men ta their destiny. He loved these stories of young men off upon the sea towards victory or despair. But for all the stories, there was never one of a young woman. I was never told what the salty sea would mean for me.

CHAPTER 14

The fall was upon us, the air cold, moist, and heavy when we neared the port city of Sundale. The call sounded as we neared and I rushed on deck with a throng of other travelers eager ta glimpse our destination. Fog rested upon the water thick as cotton, hiding away the docks like a dirty secret. Piercing up through the fog in the distance were the black jagged tops of buildings, like rotting teeth eating away the gray sky. The chimneystacks in the north spewed pillows of steam which rose only a little before falling and blending with the fog.

So terribly different from the village; from the green rolling hills and sparse houses. This was different than I had imagined it and the feeling in me chest was not of a new freedom, it was closer ta unease, as if I'd made a wretched mistake coming ta me country of birth, this foreign land. Despite me nervousness, I still desperately wanted ta know more.

Racing down below ta our tightly packed bunks, I immediately bundled meself in me best traveling coat. The docks moments away, I readied me things, wondering what the people of Victania might be like. Would they ta be so very different than the folk in the village or would they be simply people, as people are all about the earth?

Upon docking, I left with an outpouring of other wonder-struck passengers. Up we looked at the great and dark domineering brick walls in the distance. Where we stood was no less wondrous, a maze of dock-work and ships and bustling workers. All the while, me fellow passengers were led through the maze by men in blue and black uniforms.

I followed the crowd a few paces back, unsure of what ta do. The docks around me seemed ta be in chaos, but as I watched, I could see that it wasn't chaos at all. All of these crowds, which flowed hither and thither, were directed by uniformed men, lining up here, funneling there, and busy with work in between.

I walked slowly, taking all this commotion in and struggling not ta feel completely overwhelmed. A burly man wearing a frayed wool cap eyed we passengers, announcing half heartedly, "Welcome to Sundale, Victania, sir. Welcome to Sundale, ma'am."

I waited as the crowd from our ship thinned and moved on through the maze of docks where they lined up not ta far down the way. As the burly man made ta turn, I interrupted him briskly, suddenly feeling more lost and alone then ever I had felt before. "Do ya know the area?" I asked nervously.

"Sundale?" he sighed. "Aye, wha'cha lookin' fur?"

"Well, I'm—I'm not sure." I hesitated. "Not exactly."

The man let loose an annoyed grumble and said below his breath, "Barmy gimmets, never knowing shite."

"Excuse me?" I'd never heard the word 'gimmets' before, but by his tone I felt as though I'd been insulted.

"Don'cha worry yur head, eh," he shrugged off me question and though I wanted ta level an insult at his mother, I bit me tongue and listened. "There ya've got them ports, ya see?" He motioned broadly ta the ports ta the north of the passengers, flanked by ships and messy workers of all sorts, each bundled for the autumn air. "And over ta the east of there is the market. In that whole general area ya find the warehouses, fish houses, a few workers' homes, factories, that sort of thing. Not the most dangerous section of Sundale but not the safest fur the lady gimmets neither. Stay clear of it 'less ya have good reason. The men there are, eh, fiery. Get me?"

I nodded though I didn't exactly 'get him'.

"Good, ya'll thank me. Then there," he motioned in the opposite direction, "the shops continue fur a bit. Can't eat, sleep, or shite 'less ya got a dead animal abou'cha in that direction, know what I mean?"

"Dead animals?"

"Yup. And way down this way," he motioned up and over all the surrounding buildings, past the rooftops and darkened alley ways. "Ya don't want ta go that way. That's the Gin District. Foul place if ya ask me, but I don'no ya, could be ta yur likin'. But if ya want ta live through the day — and by the look of ya I'd say that ya do — then don't go in Gin District."

"The Gin District," I whispered. That was the place, the place where me Da had gone so long ago seeking a bottle of Extra Special Reserve Putrid Gin; the bottle that paid for me life. It wasn't so very far at all but a worming feeling of misgiving wriggled its way up me spine. Me head in me thoughts, I nearly missed him as he turned back ta his work, so I called out, "And what about Graendamon?"

"Eh? Ya thinkin' of being a dancer, then? Well, that's a first. Ya do have the figure fur it, don'cha? Do a little twirl for me."

"What?" I blinked, taken aback. "I will not," then added under me breath, "twirl yur mothers head…"

"Only foolin'. Don' be so serious, girl. Ya'll never be a dancer with that stick up yur bum. Graendamon is the area between the markets and the Gin District. If ya get the job, methinks I'll see ya. Welcome to Victania, girl."

Irritated, I heaved up me bag and hurried along the dock towards the city. Me heart raced in me chest as I tried ta understand the directions I had been given. For the time being, all I could do was grit me teeth and move forward.

I nearly leapt from me skin when a uniformed man in blue and black thrust a billy club before me. "I said halt woman," he shouted sternly.

"What?" I asked, a surprised hand on me heart.

"Damn gimmet, get your head out of your arse," he huffed. "Now quit eyeing me like a mule, turn round, and head to the back of the line there. This way here's for locals only. That line there," he motioned his billy club toward a crowded line of nervous looking travelers, "that line's for the gimmets."

"Why can't we walk through?" I asked confused, "And what in hell's a gimmet?"

"Inspections," he snorted. "We inspect all gimmets. You'll need your proper paperwork. You've got that don't you, your paperwork? Without it you'll be headed back home at your own expense. If you can't afford fare then you're stuck on the pier 'til you can earn it."

"I have some papers me Da gave me."

"Well, good," he responded sarcastically. "Then get in the proper line and we won't have a problem."

I walked past the line thick with people, all in traveling clothes, all nervously waiting, speaking only in hushed tones if they spoke at all. Only the children, who scuttled about amongst the feet of the rest, squealing with joy or crying in frustration.

Before me, a man held his anxious wife close, saying, "Don't worry none, we're just passing through, aren't we? We won't be in town longer than we must. They say Pristine is nice. We'll get through the line and then off we'll go, quick as a whip."

The line progressed slowly as me nervous fretting shifted ta boredom then back again. I passed the time watching the buildings lining the street a few hundred paces out of reach. The sun was burning off the morning fog, the mist rising and swirling round the small figures in the distances.

A stifled cry issued from the fore of the line and I peeked past the others as best I could, craning me neck ta see the hubbub. Through the crowd I could only catch glimpses of the scene but I could hear it and the accompanied gasps.

"You can't do this, you can't leave him here," came the desperate cries of a woman.

"Bet your arse we can," was the gruff reply. "He doesn't have the proper paperwork. I suggest you stop with your protests, unless you want to join him in the cage. Go on, say your goodbyes now, there won't be another chance. Be quick about it."

"It'll be ok," the frightened voice of a young man whispered in response. "I'll be fine."

"What can we do?"

"Unless you can go back in time and get that paperwork sorted, I'd say he's shite out of luck for now."

"No!"

"Enough, move! Move her along and take him to containment. Miss? Miss?!"

On the tips of me toes, I caught a glimpse of her red face bursting with tears, me heart twisting for her.

"For goodness sake, Miss!"

"What?!" she screamed.

"Will you be taking his things then, or leaving them here?"

"I... I..."

"Ah, forget I asked. I hope you have your effects sorted for your sake. Alright. Next!"

As they dragged the young man away towards a wooden holding cell I'd not noticed before, I began ta shake in me boots. *Good God*, thought I, *what could he have done wrong? Please, dear God, don't let anything be wrong with me papers.* I dropped me bag, loosed the string, and frantically searched for me travel papers. Me heart in me throat, I dug ever deeper unable ta find them. *I can't be stuck here!* I screamed in me mind. *I cannot be stuck on these docks so close ta the city.*

When I reached the bottom of me effects, I breathed a sigh of relief upon finding me document satchel. Me fingers shook as I flipped it open and looked through the contents. The letter of birth seemed fine enough. The letter of residence seemed ta be in order as far as I could tell. But the final paper, the letter of conduct, was meant ta have been written by another. I'd written it in a hurry, stealing me Da's signature. It had worked ta board the ship, surely it'd work again. I looked it over again and again for anything that would expose me forgery but there was nothing.

Relieved, I eased me breathing, trying ta reassure meself I'd be fine. As the line moved forward, the people behind me began ta complain about the mess I had made going through me effects. They passed me by as I crawled on me hands and knees, packing away me things.

Reaching for an article of clothing on the ground, I looked up ta see a young lad with a dirty face and clumped blond hair staring at me. He held in his hands me small jewelry box which had fallen out whilst I'd panicked. He popped it open, his eyes wide as he stared at the contents. There were only a few items within, all heirlooms left ta me by me mum, the only things she had when she died. I leaped ta snatch the box from his hands but in a flash the boy jumped back and out of the line.

"What are ya doing then?" I shouted at him. "Give it back. That's mine!"

"Not likely," said the boy before giving me a cheeky salute and bolting off along the dock.

Breaking from the line, I raced after him. "Stop him!" I shouted ta the officer in blue guiding the line. The man looked at me with a frown as he ignored the boy, letting him race pass with a chuckle. "Please! He has me things!"

"Whoa, slow down girl," the man extended his billy club ta stop me.

"Ya don't understand," said I. "He stole—"

"I understand that you're a gimmet and he's a born and bred native, isn't that right? Now, I have no obligation to protect you from a native. But I do, on the other hand, have an obligation to protect him, and the rest of the natives, from you. Now get your arse back in line before I drag you off for spite. Understand me, love?"

"What," I shouted desperately as I moved ta press past him. "He stole me Mum's—"

Violently, he wrapped his arm round me, holding me back as I struggled ta pass him. "Damn it, woman! Don't make me flog you."

I couldn't stop. Me Mum, all I had of her, was in that jewelry box. Frantically I pushed and struggled.

The pain of the blow came quick and strong. Me

eyes saw red as I fell ta the ground, and the whole of me went limp. With a cry, I lifted meself but was met with another strike ta the back of the head.

"Eh," I heard the man above me address another. "Get her to the back of the line and watch her. Restrain her if you have to."

Without dignity, I was dragged back, the pain of the blows pulsing in me head. There was no more use fighting. None at all. So I stood there, helpless. I was violated. The only part of me which connected me ta me Mum had been pulled taut and severed. The pain I felt from the beating was nauseating but the loss of me Mum was far worse.

Me arm firmly gripped by me oppressor, I watched the wood under me feet as the line slowly faded one immigrant at a time. A long while passed before I became aware enough ta think of me other effects. I had left me bag behind when I chased after the thieving boy. Me head jolted up and instantly me heart sank.

"Oh no..." I gasped.

Me bag, it was there on the dock before me lying empty. They had tore at it like scavengers, either more thieves or me fellow travelers, I knew not who.

And then, horror struck. "Me papers!"

"What?"

"Me papers, I must have me papers," I tried ta search meself, but the man jerked me arm. "Let go, damn you. I need ta find me papers!"

He looked at me bored and shrugged as he released me arm and pulled from his side a flintlock. "No matter, search away," and he leveled the weapon on me.

Frantically I felt me pockets but found nothing. "Good God, please," I whispered as I desperately glanced about the dock. "That's me bag. I need ta search me bag."

"Go," says the man, "search. I'm here with the gun, so don't go doin' something barmy."

I ran ta the empty bag and fell over it, diving me hands within, feeling about for the satchel. "No, no, no," me eyes shot wide. "This cannot be happening."

But it was so. Searching would do me no good, all had been pilfered. Slowly I rose, me breath shuddering. Not far off was the holding cell, a wooden cage filled with a few dejected souls shivering and crying, waiting ta learn what fate had in store for them. I could feel it, no matter what I could say or do, I was doomed ta suffer. I returned ta me guard, me head low, unable ta meet his eyes. "I don't have," I couldn't speak the words, they caught in me chest as I gasped for air. "I don't have anything."

"What's that?"

"Me papers, they were stolen."

"Really? Just now?"

"From me bag."

"Eh!" he shouted ta the bastard who'd bludgeoned me before. "Sir, she says her papers were stolen."

"Ah well," came the reply. "Piss poor day for her, innit." He chuckled. "No use keeping her waiting, send her to the cage won't you. Maybe she'll learn to keep a better eye on her things."

CHAPTER 15

Caged. Hopeless. Alone.

Life was often hard in our village but it was never like this. In the village, we worked for our survival. We plowed land, planted seed, harvested, fed the livestock, led it ta slaughter, butchered it ta cuts. Days were often long, sweat drenched affairs for men and women alike. And when harvest was bad, me Da would say, "And now it's time we tighten our belts. Get ready, me girl, for months of broth and a constant ache in the stomach."

Even then, when times were bad and I hadn't the energy ta make trouble for the boys, even then there were always drinks with company, stories, and games.

But now, any joy I might have savored from the village was gone.

Within the cage, I claimed a corner, curled meself

inta it, ignored the crying of the others, and simply watched the sun as it travelled over the murky sky. Slowly the day passed and the dull light of the sun, stifled by gray clouds, dipped down towards the horizon. The others held their heads in their hands and cursed their lives, but ta me their constant moaning was just noise; the aching music of captivity. After a time, the light of day had left us and our stomachs ached.

Late in the evening, after the sky turned black and all activity upon the dock melted inta stillness and the sounds of waves, a light came from the distance. Lamp light worked its way through the twisting web of docks towards us. The lamp bearer was a grizzled, uniformed man followed by a strolling man in a suit as strange as it was ornamental. As he neared, the strolling man bit inta a thick leg of chicken. He tore it apart and moaned with satisfaction, savoring it as he watched us through the bars. Me stomach grumbled painfully, me head light from a long day without food or drink.

"Nice night," said he, the chicken rolling in his mouth, flecks of it spitting toward us. "It's not raining. You lot should be thankful it's not raining. A few of you might have caught cold. Ha! Or snowing, imagine that. When it's snowing there's always the one who's frozen stiff," he lifted his arm and went rigid, miming a frozen body, then laughed as he bit inta his chicken again. "Their arms all sticking out through the bars. Ha-ha! Doesn't bother us though, does it Constable Ailey?" he slapped the chicken leg against the other mans arm.

"Nah," said the man with the lamp.

"And why is that, mate?"

"Shouldn't 'a come's why," he replied gruffly, without a hint of humor. "Bad enough here without criminal outsiders. And frankly, the gimmets deserve it. We treat ya lot too kind as it is."

"And that," said the other man, chewing as he strolled closer ta the wall of the cage separating us from him, "is absolutely correct. Too kind. Ok, ok, introductions are in order. My name is Archibald Bunker, at your service. Chief Inspector Archibald Bunker. I work for the," he chewed, his expression satisfied as he swallowed a hearty bite. "Mmmm-mmm. I work for the Chief of Foreign Affairs. I'd tell you his name, but you'll never meet him, so there really wouldn't be a point, now would there?

"You are foreign," he continued as he began ta pace, "and fortunately you were also caught attempting to enter Victania illegally. My job, among other things, is to inform you of the damn dirty predicament you have gotten yourselves into, ay. In fact, this is my favorite part of the job, I want you lot to know that, from the bottom of my heart, you are in a sticky pickle."

The grinning arsehole tossed his chicken ta the side, then leaned in with his hands on his knees as he said in a quiet tone, "But just you wait. 'Cause, you see, I don't like gimmets. You lot are ruining our country, like bone rot, eating away at the fabric of society from within. If it were up to me — and very soon it will be — I'd strap a cannon ball to your feet, toss you over the side of the dock, and have done with you.

"But," he shouted as he stood and resumed his pacing, "for now, that's not the case. For now, we must follow the rules at hand, and I am obliged to tell you how you can extradite yourself from this situation."

Extradite? I struggled ta understand the word, but I knew well enough not ta speak.

"P-please sar," a man cried. "I duna do enythan' wrong. I—"

"Didn't do anything wrong?" said the chief inspector. "Did I understand you right? Sometimes I can hardly tell that we are speaking the same language. Didn't do anything wrong. Well then, that must have been our mistake, we must let you go immediately."

He nodded ta the door, and Constable Aiely grinned as he unlocked it and cracked it open, pulling a flintlock and leveling it on him. "Just you," he said.

The man who'd protested began ta quiver, shaking his head vigorously. "No, I'm sarry, no, no—"

"Yes," said the constable, wagging the gun.

The man trudged forward with unsure steps as we all watched in silence. Out of the cage, he stood there unable ta meet the eyes of either constable. And then he began ta cry, first a tear, then a shiver, and then a burst of nervous sobs.

Chief Inspector Bunker neared him, his eyes level on him. Then, pausing ta look over his shoulder and back down the docks, he looked ta Aiely who nodded. With a sudden *crack* Bunker smacked a billy club from his side against the poor man's jaw. The man yelped and crumpled ta the ground in a heap. Bunker raised up his billy club then hammered it down and between each strike bellowed, "We!" *thud*, "Don't!" *thud*, "Make!" *thud*, "Mistakes!"

Horrified, we gathered in the back of the cage, unable ta look away from the savage beating. A woman clutched me shoulder and began ta sob.

Breathing heavily, Chief Inspector Bunker rose up and looked at us. For a moment his eyes met mine, eyes without remorse. "Who was he? A rapist come to ravage our women? A serial killer come to strike fear in our hearts? A sniveling con artist come to steal our livelihoods? An anti-national come to spread his hate? They've all come here. I've seen the havoc they can wreck and I will not let them into our country again! Shite! Ailey, hand me your neckerchief, I've got blood on my gloves."

After wiping his gloves clean, Chief Inspector Bunker walked ta the cage and this time as he paced he dragged the billy club against the rattling bars. "If there is ever something wrong," he said, speaking more ta himself than ta us, "we spot it. If we slacken our resolve, if we don't adhere to the rules, then the evils of the world slip within our borders. Victania must be protected, our citizens must be protected and if I was to show you mercy, by letting you in, and you were to harm one of our people, I would be to blame. And rightly so. But that doesn't happen anymore because I don't let it happen. I'm sure you understand.

"But," he said, the billy club rattling against the bars, "for now there is a way out. Rather than punish you, our superiors have deemed it prudent to simply not let you enter the country. Starting tonight, you live on the docks and are simply not being allowed entry onto Victanian soil. If you have money, you can buy entry onto a barge and head back home or to anywhere else you like. If you do not have money, you can gain employment on a ship or on the docks performing day labor or whatever work you can scrounge up. Then you, too, can go back home. Meanwhile, my men will be watching you diligently. It's a terrible waste of resources, so crimes committed on the docks will be handled most harshly.

"Well now," he said taking a breath and

straightening his over-sized collar, "that leaves one last thing. Your clothes will need to come with me, so off they get. There are men coming now with your own special attire that you will wear at all times upon the docks."

"I won't undress for ye," a frightened woman next ta me shook as she clutched at herself.

Chief Archibald Bunker eyed daggers at her. "You will," he said venomously. "Do you know why? Because it will be most uncomfortable if you force my men to do it for you." Then he smiled, bowed, and said, "Best of luck with your current misfortunes," before he turned and left.

CHAPTER 16

The gray woolsacks they called clothes were brought ta us in a stiff heap, and there in the cage on the dock, officers watched, hands on muskets, as we dressed. The uniforms, made of gnarled wool with fibers sticking out, itched terribly. I kept me eyes ta the ground, a fire burning in me; a deep and searing hatred for these men. I wanted ta kill them, a dark sensation I'd never in me life felt before.

In the darkness, we were led away in a line, one guard before us, one guard behind and both armed, directing us gruffly. Rough against me skin, the uniform rubbed raw every sensitive part of me, forcing me ta pull the fabric away from me chest as we walked.

Upon a pier was a small bunkhouse. As we entered I glimpsed the quiet watching eyes of prisoners who came before us. Some had matted hair, thick like ropes. Some had rotten teeth, jagged like broken glass stained brown. And though some seemed western, others eastern, and still others more exotic, all their skin were hues of darkness, turned leather brown, rusty red, or charcoal black from long days exposed upon the docks.

Amongst the rows, I found an empty bunk and laid meself down, curling inta meself, ignoring the world. The fire in me chest roared, a desire ta punish those who'd done me wrong this day. But it was a useless fire, I was a powerless girl, lost, starved, and couldn't even find some comfort upon the planks that were called me bed. The fire raged and me skin grew hot, and then in a sudden, silent burst the swell in me chest poured from me eyes in streams of hot tears.

"Hello," came a deep whisper from a man on the bunk above mine.

"I'm sorry," said I. "I didn't mean ta disturb—"

"Do not fret," he replied, speaking slow and in an unusual accent. "First day, rough. Days pass, feel less. What is name?"

"I'd rather just keep ta meself," I said through a flow of fresh tears.

"Mm," he said, then shifting in his bed above me he added, "I understand."

He didn't speak the rest of the night through. All that could be heard was the quiet crying of the newly imprisoned, and all that could be felt was the cold air against me falling tears.

When first light broke, with its haze leaking through a few empty window holes, I crawled off the plank board bunk, stiff and hungry. I had nothing, not even the remains of me travel sack. Me gut twisted in a noisy and wretchedly painful way. It should not have surprised me that our captors felt no obligation ta feed us.

Looking out along the twisting docks, I saw the peppering of uniformed men sprinkled here and there, watching us warily. I came ta learn that these were a special branch of the constables: the foreign affairs officers.

Unsure of what ta do, I listened ta the other foreigners for some clue, desperate for any way ta find food. The woman with sun worn skin stayed behind in the bunkhouse and the newer arrivals huddled in their own corner watching them. "Save yurself a lot of trouble," one weary woman spoke ta two of the ladies who'd been held in the cage with me. "Only one way we survive on the docks, better get used ta the idea of lying with strangers. It's a dog snog dog world, and dogs that don't snog don't eat."

I left those regrettable women behind and watched the men as they walked off in silence. They walked like slaves, their wool uniforms hanging loose from their bodies as if they hadn't had a proper meal in months. Most worked their way north, past lines of fishing boats piled high with netting, and I followed.

"Zey von't let ya vork, miss," said a bald man who had bristling hair pouring out his ears.

"Course they will," I replied.

"I tellin' ya, miss, ya best ta turn back round. I seen it before, a voman like ya vanting to avoid it. But, miss, I'm tellin' ya it can't be done. Ya as likely ta get beat for asking. I seen it, a girl beat for it. She die only ze next day. Zey won't let vomen vork on the docks."

"There must be something I can do. I'll gut fish all day and all night if they just feed me something."

"Zat bad, eh?" the man asked with a knowing nod. "Hm. Take this. I know how it gets." From his pocket he pulled a hard, crumbling piece of bread and handed it ta me. "Zis get ya by for day at least."

I hesitated. Had it really come ta this? It was ta fast. Only a day ago I was a passenger. Now what was I? Cursed methinks. I took the bread and dug me teeth past the stiff crust and inta the dusty meat of it. It fell apart like dirt in me mouth but I forced meself ta swallow.

Upon reaching the entry to the fishing docks, the men approached a small booth with a makeshift sign that read "DAY LABOR," each being directed down a different path as I nervously watched and waited for me turn.

"Excuse me," said I trying ta keep strength in me voice. "I'm looking for work, anything."

"What?" said the burly man behind the booth wrapped in a wool coat. Waving a dismissive hand, he scoffed, "Yur not serious? Off with ya!"

"Please, I need ta work—"

"Then go elsewhere," he replied. "Men only."

"I can do it—"

"I donna care what ya can do, gimmet," he sighed, rubbing his forehead. "Men only. Now get before I need ta get serious, get me?"

In desperation I reached out ta him and he brushed me arm away. "I need ta eat," I pleaded. "I've got nothing! Everything I had was stolen. I'll work for it. I'll do anything for it, please! I don't care what it is. Give me the job no one else will do, so long as ya give me some food?"

The man glared at me for a long, silent moment. "I'm tempted ta say," he mused, glancing over his shoulder then back at me with a thoughtful look. "I'm tempted ta say, that ain't none of my problem. But ya look awl right, an' it's been a dry week. Hm, well, perhaps we can come to some arrangement. Stick 'round here a moment love, mayhap I can help ya out."

A wave of relief washed over me as I clasped me

hands together and thanked the man.

"Just wait here," he said and turned away.

In the cold I waited. I looked about me, at the shabby wood shacks at the end of the piers, at the ships sailing off in the distance, and at the warehouses in the direction the man had left. A tall fence ran along the border between this strange dock town and the city, as if we were in a different world altogether.

As I looked about, I caught sight of a foreign affairs officer leaning against a small hut not far off, his eyes focused intently on me. A strip of water separated us but the way he eyed me made me feel as if he were only inches away, staring me down. Our eyes connected and he didn't flinch, just fixed upon me a dangerous expression. When the man from behind the booth returned with a friend, I was a little comforted ta not be alone in the sight of that foreign affairs officer anymore.

"Follow me, love," said the man behind the booth as he turned and walked within a fenced off area. "This way, it's time for ya ta earn yur first meal."

I nodded, thanking him again and following him with a last look behind me as the officer stood and slowly began ta walk down the dock.

I was led through a busy dock-way, as laborers and sailors bustled all about us, towards a warehouse separated from the mainland by the tell-tale high fence. The smell of fish was strong and when he led me towards the warehouse, the entry gaping wide with a waterway wide enough for a large boat ta enter it, the smell grew to nearly overpowering. The man paused before a door ta a side room, then looked back ta me and said, "Here we are, lovely."

I halted and looked at him suspiciously. "What sort of work do ya need from me then?" I asked eyeing the doorway. Something tasted foul in the air but me suspicions were tempered by me hunger.

"The kind that puts food on yur plate, love," he said dryly. "Are ya coming or not."

Taking a cautious step, I peeked through the door. With a hand on me back, he gently pushed me forward inta the room. It was the touch that caused understanding ta first strike me with a sudden panic. I should have seen it sooner but me mind wasn't right. "No," I gasped and tried ta stop. "No, I don't think—"

"Oh for shites sake!" He cursed as he gruffly grabbed me arm, pulling me through the door and slamming it behind us with a loud thud. Me heart shot ta racing as I pulled frantically ta get away but his grip was strong and forceful. With a great yank, he whipped me before him, the room a blur and a stiff pain in me side erupted from slamming against something. I twisted round, struggling ta keep his face in view. His arm on me, he stepped forward. I lashed out at him with me free hand, clawed at his face, felt the skin of him, the stubble. Three streaks of red ran along his forehead.

Hand on his face, he shouted, "Calm down won'cha, girl! Ya telling me this ain't what ya wanted? Yur gimmets, ain't cha? Ya got family near? Ya got anybody ta take care of ya? 'Cause if ya don't, this is it, love. Yur as good as a whore already. Best to get used ta it early, mayhap ya'll be able to fill that belly of yurs, eh. But ya keep fighting me like that, there won't be any food for ya at the end, get me!"

"Bugger off!" I shouted back.

With a bitter frown, he shoved me backwards, sending me sprawling against the edge of a table as he approached.

"First time's always the hardest, love," he smiled, a dribble of blood running down his forehead and inta his eyebrow. "Trust me."

I scrambled back around the table but with me back ta the wall there was nowhere ta go. He moved in quick and smacked me hard. The world a stinging fog, I desperately looked about for anything, but filling me view was only the man before me — arms with taut muscles, his bear like hands reaching out.

I gasped. Me palms slipped against the entrails of fish upon the table as I reached ta pull meself up and over. Then I felt it against the edge of me finger, the long, thin filleting knife. His fingers dug roughly inta me thigh. He dragged me back, I snatched at the knife and I was under him. With the effort of pulling me closer, he leaned over me, his stubble gray, his long black hair speckled with streaks of silver. His eyes were blue and they saw the knife. In an instant I flung me arm round him and with all of me weight, I buried the whole of the thin knife down, cutting skin, blade rubbing against bone, deep inta the nape of his neck.

"Love?" he breathed as the knife peaked out his throat. Flecks of blood upon his lip.

"I ain't yur love," I sputtered, me hands shaking violently, me eyes wide with animal rage. I began ta cry furiously as I pulled the knife free and with a sudden primal scream I buried the blade inta him again. The blood bubbled from the gouge in his neck, raining down on me.

I heaved at his heavy body, his hair hanging down, droplets falling, pattering upon me face. "No, no, no, no," me eyes were wide as I watched his concerned eyes flickering about. Then pause, wide. And the last breath was breathed.

"Oh God!" With all me might, I pushed the heavy man's limp body off of me — me palms, red. "Oh God. Oh no." I wiped me running nose with the back of the shivering gray wool sleeve as I looked about, trying ta figure a way out of this horrible turn.

Hurrying ta the door, I cracked it open and peaked through. I saw the still busy docks moving on undeterred, unaware of the murder I had committed, of the man dead upon the floor, and of me, the girl with hands sticky with blood. I began ta shut the door when a piqued face in the distance caught me eye. Leaning against the entry ta the warehouse was the foreign affairs officer who had been watching me so intently earlier and his eyes rested upon the sliver of me exposed face through the crack in the door. I quickly pushed it shut, but as I did I caught a glimpse of the man righting himself and walking in me direction.

Me hands shook terribly as I backed away from the door. When me heels touched the body, I nearly jumped from me skin. *What had I done? I'd done murder in a cruel and foreign land. What was I ta do now?* There would be no mercy, not for me, nothing was more certain. Looking about the room for an escape, I found a small window high on the wall and darted for it.

The latch jostled and the door was pushed open. I froze as a face appeared in the doorway. He spoke as he entered, but ta me it was not but noise. He froze when he saw me, when he saw the red speckled about me face, me shirt wet with blood. He glared at me like I was sin. And then, as he saw the man, dead, blood pooling about him, there in the door his face flashed with anger, and he scowled at me like I was the devil.

I was already turning, scrambling up, and forcing meself through the small window.

A shrill call of a whistle rang sharp, and with me top half out the window, all I could see were the busy docks and the sky and the ocean beyond. I panicked as me hips caught against the frame, and as I struggled, the pressure of a hand beat at me ankle. I kicked furiously as I roughly pulled me hips through and fell headlong ta the other side. Landing hard, I gasped for air, but me chest refused ta pull it in. With an effort I rose, eyes wet with tears, face hot, and as I started forward, I pulled at the air, gagging with the effort of it, forcing it through with will alone inta me lungs.

I glanced over me shoulder as I stumbled on and the face of the foreign affairs officer, filled with rage, appeared at the window. He stuck his arm through and tried ta climb as I had, but cursed when his broad shoulders would not manage. "I'll get you girl," he hissed, eyes square on me. "Before the day is done, I'll see your damn dirty head separated from your filthy gimmets body, you murdering piece of utter shite!"

But I was running. A shot rang out behind me and I yelped, terrified.

"Quick! Someone's been killed!" The muted call followed me from within the walls, nearly drowned in the clopping of me feet against the dock.

Me boots were not made for running, the heels slipped against the wet wood as I slid about —

huffing through me cries, desperate ta put as much distance between the warehouse and meself as possible.

Through the gate and under the sign that read "DAY LABOR," I ran. Then without warning, a force struck me and I plummeted ta the grounds, arms wrapping round me, pinning me down.

"No! Please!" I shouted.

"What have you done now, traitorous bitch!"

"Ya don't understand!"

Another scowling face upon me, the other man from the day labor stand, his nose red from the cold.

Struggling, trying ta right meself, I fought against him in vain, helpless and despairing, crying and cursing. But even as me soul shrank, a shadow rose over us and I heard a hollow thud. The man upon me fell ta the ground and was quickly dragged ta the side. Over me stood a dark man, skin darker than any shade I had ever seen in me life. Dressed in gray, hair like a black halo, he looked down at me from over the man's limp body as he stepped closer, holding a spinning thing in his hand. "Sock and rocks," he said, and I recognized the voice from the night previous. "Useful in bad times. Come," and he lowered his hand ta me, glancing over his shoulder. "Come, we run, now."

Pulling me ta me feet, he held me wrist hard and darted off, tugging me along with him down the docks. There was no other course ta take. Rounding a corner, we fell on the far side of a stack of crates. "In." He lifted an empty crate with the bottom removed. "You hide. Quick! No noise, do not leave. I come back, later. Ok?" His face twisted as he fought for words, then he looked at me as if searching for understanding.

I nodded and crawled under the crate. "What about ya?" I asked.

"Not me," he said as he lowered the crate, blocking out the light of day. "Just you."

Alone in the dark I sat curled, me arms clutching round me knees. Me heart pounded with such a force that the blood pulsing through me arms was painful. Every breath sounded like a scream and as the sound of boots against wood and muffled voices neared, I was sure me breath would get me discovered. They shouted angrily and I shuddered, holding me breath, attempting not ta brush the edge of the crate walls as I trembled.

Then the sounds grew faint and soon only the shouting in the distance could be heard. Even so, for a long while I dared not move. I let me frightened tears fall and did not brush them away. Hours passed but time was no comfort. With each moment came new dreads. Tense hours I waited, at times wondering if I should try ta escape but then the sounds would come near again. So I waited. Waited for the dark man who'd led me ta safety.

I waited, huddled, crying, silent, and alone.

CHAPTER 17

I had fallen inta a terrified daze by the time the docks finally went quiet. Footsteps clopped upon the dock, drawing near, shaking me out of me stupor, and causing panic ta take hold. Then the crate lifted. First a sliver and I held me breath, then a gap and I readied meself for the fight, and finally I saw the shadow of a dark man in the cloudless night.

"Hello," he said, voice deep, face black with shadow. I blinked, clearing from me eyes the darkness of me hiding place, forcing me eyes ta adjust ta the light of the stars. When I saw me hands, the palms, which were once red, were now stained brown.

"How are you?" said the man as he lowered a hand for me ta take and helped me up. The dock around us was empty but for the stacks of crates and cargo here, blocking us from the sight of anyone on the far side.

In the opposite direction was an endless dark sea, the rolling waters twinkling on the peaks of gentle waves as they caught the starlight. The waters lapped against the beams of the docks. These sounds had been me only companion as I waited the full day and inta the night inside the little wooden box. Now that I saw the waves, the ocean, the vastness and darkness of the sparkling seascape, it felt more like a prison than a companion. The ocean was a prison keeping me here in this ugly country, keeping me away from me home I had foolishly left. More than anything I felt stupid and ashamed.

"It's all gone so wrong," I whispered, watching the point in the distance where the water disappeared inta the sea of stars on the horizon.

"Yes," the man said and I found meself startled again by him, by the way his features were so like the darkness. I'd never seen a man this dark before, though me Da had told me of the peoples of Africa many times. "We are safe now but not long time. No bunks, you understand? They watch bunks. There is no going back."

I nodded. Tears were welling up in me raw eyes and each time a tear fell, the pain of it upon me skin felt like a rash rubbed with sand. Wiping the tears away only made them worse so I let them cling ta me eyes, dangle, then painfully fall. "They want ta kill me," I said through shuddering breaths. "I heard them say it, talkin' about stringing me up against the bunkhouse and letting me die slow. But they don't know I was just... He came at me, I had no choice—"

"Shhhhh," the man breathed, a finger ta his lips. "I understand. I was close. You walked north this morn' and I knew bad things were gonna happen." Placing a hand on either one of me shoulders, he studied me for a moment, then whispered, "We sit for now. You calm." He nodded and helped lower me ta the ground. "Sorry, my speech. I still learning Victanian. What is you name?" he asked.

"Yevylin," I replied, wiping me nose. "I mean, Miss Over. Miss Yevylin Over."

"Where you come from?" His voice was deep, calm and soothing.

"Nowhere," I said and laughed despite meself. "Nowhere anyone has ever heard of."

"I understand," he nodded. "I am Bheka. We are the same," he smiled and, taking my hand, he pointed ta me palm. "Africa, yes? Here is top, north. Here is bottom, south. I from here," he pointed ta the middle of me pinkie. "Zimbabwe," he said.

Me back went rigid as the clicking of heels against the dock clopped in the distance. We looked ta one another and he put a finger ta his lips. Peering round the edge of the crates, we anxiously watched a halo of lamplight move down the way slowly — *clop, clop, clop*

111

— until behind some structure or fence the halo faded and the sound melted away.

"Shouldn't we go?" I asked. "We must find some place ta hide. We should do something."

"No place to go." Pointing ta the spot where we sat hunched, he said, "This where we hide. Then we must escape. Escape the dock. We escape or we die, yes?" I could hardly see his expression in the dark but he sounded confident.

"But how?" I asked

"First you must calm," and he stressed the word. Pulling something from his pocket, he handed it ta me, cold and soft with a rough skin. "Here, eat. Potato. Eat now, then we escape. Yes? Tell me, why you here? Why Victania?"

Without hesitation, I dove inta the cold potato, tearing it apart, the food deliciously painful as it filled me famished stomach. When I could breathe no more, I paused in me ravishing and slowed ta chew properly. "Family, I s'pose," said I through a mouth half full.

"Ah," he replied, and the look on his face was grim. "Family. If family here, why they not help?"

I forced a large swallow down, savoring even the way the lump of it struggled down me throat. "Do you have water?" I asked.

"Yes." He produced a small wooden flask and handed it ta me.

The water I guzzled and the moisture of it so relieved me parched throat, it was as though the water was turning paper back inta flesh. "Me family's not here," I replied, wiping the water from me mouth with me rough sleeve. "No help for me," then I added, "well, except ya. Thank ya for helping me."

"Yes," he nodded. "Again, we are da same. I also am here for family. See dis?" He pulled from his pocket a shard, brilliantly white even in the dim starlight. He held it reverently as he showed it ta me. It was a knife, all of it a single piece, all pearly and aglow. "Ivory," he said as if explaining the entire mystery of the thing.

"Oh." Confused by it, I sipped on me water and tried ta think of a response, saying lamely, "Pianos. Piano keys."

He looked at me strangely for a moment, as if the very mention of a piano was insulting, then slipped the glistening shard back inta a pocket. "Yes," he nodded solemnly, "Piano keys. You know about ivory? About piano keys?"

"As much as there is ta know. They use ivory ta make the keys," I shrugged.

"And my people?"

"Yur people?" I asked, confused.

He frowned, searching for the words but then only said, "Zimbabwe."

"I'm sorry," I said and sipped at the last of the

water, exhaustion suddenly taking hold of me with a force. "Thanks for the water and food. I don't know how much longer... As it is, I don't feel so good."

"How you feel?" he said, looking concerned. Placing a hand against me forehead, he added, "We must go soon."

"Yes," I nodded, my head feeling heavy and partially drunk. "But how? They are patrolling the docks, looking for us."

"Yes," he said, "No escape on docks. People all times watching. We must swim."

"Swim!" I nearly shouted. "We can't swim. It's ice cold."

"Yes," he nodded. "Dangerous. Listen. Guards block city, many are there watching. They find you, they kill you. String you up, as you say. So, we swim. Is cold, yes. Much cold. That way," he pointed, "far south, there we find a hole, yes? I hear tale in bunks, they say there is hole. They say some swim, they swim south and they escape, crawl in hole, find way in city. Only way. Dangerous, yes. Guards hear water, guards bring musket, shoot. Water is cold, you get cold, you drown. Dangerous, but only way." I sat baffled, but not conscious enough ta protest. He then added, "This," he tugged at his gray uniform, "This is good. This will keep you warm in water."

I was nodding, listening ta the words even as understanding them slipped from me. "And ya'll

114

come with me?" was all I could think ta ask.

"Yes," he replied.

"But why?"

"Why?"

"Why are ya helping me?"

"Ah," for a moment he went quiet as he watched me intently. "You look like someone," he said slowly. "Little bit. When you come in bunkhouse, I see you and somehow you look…" he trailed off, turned away from me ta look out at the endless ocean. "You look like my sister."

"Yur sister?"

He shrugged, adding, "Not hair, skin or strength, just eyes." He held two fingers close together and added, "Little bit. Only dis much."

CHAPTER 18

Peering over the edge of the dock, all was darkness and shadow. I couldn't see the water below. Only the sound of it, the gentle rolling waves against the beams, gave any proof that there was water below us at all.

"We just jump?" I asked. Me head light, I struggled ta stay focused. The sky above us was slowly getting consumed by a great sweeping cloud rolling in from over the ocean in the distance, blocking out the stars bit by bit.

"Yes," Bheka whispered. "No noise. No splash. No sound. Be silent. Stay close. No speak until we are away from docks. Yes?"

"Yes." I shivered, me skin awaiting the icy waters.

The clouds ate the sky ever more and the hum of rain began ta drone in the distance. Bheka's shadow leaned over the edge. He lowered himself slowly down, hung, then dropped. I watched him fall, disappearing inta the darkness, and though he had fallen far, the splash was muffled by the waves and the encroaching rain.

"I just need ta hang and let go," I said ta meself nervously as I followed Bheka's example. "No noise. Not unless I want ta be, eh, strung up."

Biting me lip, I turned round, me feet over the edge. How had this all gone so wrong? Me palms flat against the damp wood, me stomach likewise, I let me legs hang and gasped at me own actions. "No," I whispered, then pulled at the slick wood. "No, I can't do this. I can't—" But in a terrible joke of fate, me hands slid, me body fell, and I twisted helplessly in the air. A yelp escaped me lips just as me back slammed against the water.

The bitter cold rushed over me, the foul taste of the ocean filled me mouth, stinging me nose. The shock of the cold forced me body ta try and suck in air but I was under water and instead only breathed in the ocean. Panicking, I scrambled for the surface, for air. Me head breached the water and instantly I began ta painfully hack up the ocean I had breathed.

Bheka swam ta me, wrapped me in his arms. "Breathe," he whispered. "Breathe."

Sounds upon the docks, a scurrying, and me back went rigid. Calls were shouted, the hurried clopping of feet neared. "We must go, now," he whispered, fear plain in his voice. "Quick!"

Me lungs burning, the water biting, we swam hard, slipping under the docks, weaving between beams with our hands feeling their way through the darkness. Me feet stroked seaweed as we swam and each time it brushed me legs I panicked a little more, swam a little harder. The cold took me and me feet numbed. The harder I swam, the weaker I felt, and the more difficult it was ta keep me head above water. *This will be it*, thought I. *Soon I'll freeze, lose strength, and sink like a weight ta the bottom of the ocean ta drown quietly and alone.*

Lamplight erupted from above us, casting a yellow glow from the docks above ta the waters beyond.

"Do you see them?" A man shouted.

"Not yet, we'll find her now though. Last mistake that bloody whore will ever make."

"The boat should be coming round soon."

"Over there, double-quick to the far south side. I want as many as you can spare watching south, and if you see that murderous bitch, just shoot her and let the boats dredge her up. We will get her tonight, no excuses!"

"Yes sir. You heard him boys, quickly now."

A company of men above us ran, their footsteps growing faint.

"Did anyone call Chief Inspector Bunker?"

"Not yet, sir."

"Good. Go and get him, but not too quick, understand. I want her body on deck before he gets here."

"Yes, sir."

Another man left.

Then a whisper came, not more than a muttering. "I'll get you girl," the man on the dock growled under his breath. "I want to see the look on your face when you die. I want your gimmets death mask. Just try getting away a second time. Just try it."

Bheka turned ta face me, a finger upon his lips, then whispered in me ear, "Do you hear?"

I nodded, kicking me feet ta stay afloat and holding me body tight ta try ta keep a modicum of warmth.

"If we go south, they will see," he whispered. "They must know. I do not know a different way. South is the only way."

"What do we do," me teeth chattered.

After a moment of thought, he said, "I will swim out into the water. They will see me. Then I go back. You no move until they follow me, then you go south. Only way."

"No," I whispered, but he had already turned, already began swimming hard for the south side of the intertwining docks. I struggled in the water after him, hearing meself yelling, "No!"

Ahead of us the light cast from up above dimly met the water and just before reaching it Bheka dove under, disappearing from view. In the center of the light, he burst forth, spun back round, and swam back under the dock. The *crack!* of musket fire rang out thrice in short time.

"She's slipping away," someone shouted from above. "Over here, quick now!"

"Watch between these docks, and you inform the others. Where's the bloody boat?"

He reached me panting and, pulling me close, he whispered, "Do not move from here awhile." He looked at me as if there was more ta say but then turned away and swam out, away from the docks and toward the open sea. Shivering from the cold, my shaking hand reached out for him.

"There she is, barmy woman is swimming out inta the ocean."

"Shoot her, damn it!"

Shots sounded and I clutched desperately at a beam covered in sharp barnacles. Tears ran down me face as I watched Bheka disappear inta the night. I clutched ta the beam and the barnacles cut at me hands, the salt in the waters bringing a sharp sting ta the small cuts. Watching out inta the water, a pit formed in me heart for this man I hardly knew. I peered ta find him but already he was out of sight, shot, drown, or perhaps still swimming on.

I waited as the activity bustled, watched as a small boat rowed out and searched the waters. Me body had grown tired and numb, just a constant ache in the back of me brain ta remind meself that I could still feel pain. When I could no longer take it, I slowly swam away.

The clouds from the distance had finally reached us, cutting away the light of the stars and pouring upon me an angry rain.

I swam along a great rock wall rising up from the ocean where the waves crashed. With a hand against the rocks, I swam slowly until exhaustion struck me. Clinging ta a stone ta stay afloat, the waves rushed over me head as I struggled ta rest, gasping for air as they pulled away. For a moment I attempted ta climb but me numb fingers could not grip the edges between the stones. Me arms grew tired, me teeth chattering, me eyes blinking away the rain and the assaulting sea water. I moved on unable ta see before me, keeping me hand along the wall as I swam, feeling about for the rumored hole Bheka had spoken of.

With each stone, I reached onward, pulled meself forward, struggled ta keep me muscles working, ta keep me eyes open. Near despair, a foul, rotten stench reached out ta welcome me as the water thickened. I gagged as I moved forward and finally came across it, the gurgling hole. Rusting bars that had once blocked the entrance had long ago been eaten away by the sludge. The jagged edges of the bars jutted viciously out of the putrid waters like teeth as the sickening contents of the city spewed forth.

Mechanically, I passed between the teeth, the rotting bars rubbing hard against me legs. There was nothing left ta feel, no emotion, no fear, just mindless moving on, just a flickering hope that this rotten path would save me. I found me footing upon the slippery brick floor within and waded through the mess, nauseous from the stink, and exhausted. When I finally met a platform, I pulled meself up and out of the filth, then pressed on until I found the first exit, a ladder rising up like the path saving sinners from hell. Except heaven was Sundale, the same city who'd locked me away on the docks ta die.

Upon the streets, I shuffled weakly, shivering cold, starving, and afraid. And then, ta weary ta continue, I curled meself up in a ball and leaned against a wall where I slowly began ta sleep a troubled, quaking sleep. In the back of me mind I knew that without help I would not survive the night, but I was so tired.

CHAPTER 19

"And then I woke up," I said to The Missus, nodding with an awkward sense of finality. I knew not the time, but surely it was past midnight and still she watched me with that piercing gaze. During the telling, when I had glanced up at her, I caught her studying me, focused on my every blink, every twitch of the lips, every instantaneous expression which might betray something. As the night wore on, I had come to realize that listening to my story wasn't really what this meeting was about at all, as I had thought it was. It was about measuring me. But by the time this notion had struck, I was too tired to care, to worn to change my tactics. Weary, I just wanted to know whether this night I would have a bed and a blanket, so I closed my story quickly and waited for her response.

"That's me story," I said in my village's peculiar accent. "That's it."

"After you woke," she began matter-of-factly, "one of my girls found you then led you to Miss Bottoms who in turn led you to me, correct?"

"Yes," I said nervously.

"Hm." She tapped her finger against her lips as she watched me intently.

I was still exhausted from the days previous, my muscles still aching, my head dizzyingly light. Had this been any other situation, had The Missus been any other woman, I would be fighting to stay awake. But not here, not with her. With her eyes on me, my skin tingled and my mind remained more or less alert. A brain wrapped gently in wire has a hard time sleeping.

"It was an interesting story," she said after some time. "I have no way of knowing at this time how much of it is true but it feels honest enough. I liked the bit about the man, when you dove your knife into him a second time for good measure." She pulled a pipe from the table and packed it as she spoke. "That's the animal inside you, maybe a tiger, or in your case maybe a kitten just learning she has claws. It doesn't matter. The point is that our society has trained woman to take what they are given. You've seen the whores in the streets, no doubt. Or the sad whores on the docks, in any case."

"Yes."

"Tell me this, are any of them men?"

"No, of course not."

"Of course not," she repeated. "And it is that very sentiment, that very 'of course' that I take issue with. Not with you, my good girl, with society as a whole. That's what we're talking about now, Miss Over, if you'll indulge me. Society. Do you not see the issue here? Those women, those whores out there, suffering through rain and snow and bastards of men who return them broken more times than I care to count, they didn't set out to be whores. As young girls, they didn't rest on their mothers laps and dream about the many men they would appease in order to buy bread, clothes, food, and lodging. They were women like you, and judging by the story of your birth, probably closer to you than you might care to admit.

"I hate to say it darling," she continued, "but those whores are your people, and just like you this past week, they've been beaten down by circumstance. At one point they had to fight but they gave in. That's where you're different, Miss Over. That's where we, Scarlets, are different. We don't give in. We find a way to get what we need, practically if possible, violently if necessary. We've not bought into the idea that we are lower beasts, bred to docilely follow the rules. Oh, when backed into a corner those whores will certainly bare their teeth and make a lot of noise. But women like us, we use the corner to our advantage, as a stepping stone to greater things. Do you know why?"

"No," I said quietly, vaguely wondering what the word 'docilely' meant.

"Because women like us, Miss Over, have realized that we can have power too," The Missus said with a grin. "I'm not talking about some metaphysical idea of power," she waved a hand in the air dismissively. "We can have physical power, economic power, social power, power to shape the outcome of our own lives. When you become a Scarlet, circumstance comes and goes, and when it gets rough we take it by the bullocks and squeeze it into submission.

"There is a spark of that in you." Her eyes alight, she spoke with a glinting passion. "Now the question is, can you take that spark and set it to tinder? I think you can. You fought, killed a man outright, and bravo for that. I'll be looking into it, of course, but supposing you're story was true, he was a pig and he deserved it. Do you feel regret for killing him?"

Startled by the question, the image of it filled my mind's eye like a horrific dream, so vivid, the blood as it pattered upon my face. "Yes," I said.

"A butcher feels no regret for killing pigs, Miss Over. In any case, we Scarlets aren't fighting to save ourselves from society, we are fighting to put a knife to society's neck and make it behave the way we damn well feel like it should. I can see the taxidermy headpieces, the ornate dresses, the caviar and boiler-carriages that a few women have and we know how they got it. They latched like a leech onto the right husband and that husband exploited thousands. I can see that and it sickens me. Let those prissy leaching women rot, we don't need them. Rob the exploitative husbands blind and leave them sterile. What Scarlets need are women who are strong enough to fight for what they believe in. We're not fighting just for things but for a new world order.

"So," she paused and brought her pipe to her lips, "now is the time for the question, but before I ask I'll let you know how this, your situation, might unravel. First, you can answer the question correctly and you'll become an understudy, an initiate so to speak. You won't be a Scarlet, not for a good long while, not till you prove yourself. You'll do the shite work, the nasty jobs, play the whole game. That is option one.

"Next, sweetie, is option two. You don't become an understudy. Fine. We have bunkhouses where women like you can sleep. We offer protection for those women, but it's not free. You'll be expected to earn money on your own—I don't care how—and you'll be expected to pay for our services. You won't ever come in contact with me again, or if you do it won't be a pleasant exchange. That's option two.

"Then there's the third option," she continued. "We send you back out on the streets. You die an ugly death in short order. That's not a threat, that's just the way it goes. Without us, my money isn't on you making a long while before you're picked up by the foreign affairs officers, either to die publicly on the docks or to rot in jail.

"So here's the question, deary: do you see the dirt before you and a plate of gold just out of reach? Do you see a world where wealth is lorded over you while you suffer in filth, grime, and back breaking work? Do you thirst for another way, a better way, a way where you can be part of a new ruling class?"

"Yes," I breathed, caught up in the vision of it.

"And are you willing to work with your sisters in arms to take the world by the bullocks and make that bastard behave? In other words, when it comes down to it, deary, will you kill again to change the world? For your sisters? For yourself? After all, and trust me on this, deary, your sisters will kill, and much more, for you."

My breathing stopped, the only sound was that of blood rushing behind my ears and the noise of the crowd in the pub below us. I could picture myself back in our village, working in the house, watching other people's lives pass by while mine had remained ever the same. Da was the only thing that had mattered but he was gone. I had less than nothing, not even an identity.

I remembered the stories Da used to tell me,

stories of all sorts: of adventure, of loves won and lost, of peril and turmoil and tragedy, and here I was without a story of my own. But now I was in Sundale, the city where I was born, one of the most modern and vile cities on the planet. This was my chance to make a difference for myself. As The Missus said it, to make a difference for the world, or so I truly believed.

I swallowed hard, my chest a flutter as the word rose up and passed my lips, "Yes."

"Then say it," she said wryly.

"I will... will kill to change the world."

"Oh, come now, say it with gusto or not at all. This is a declaration, Miss Over!"

I shouted, "I will kill to change the world!"

"One last time, love."

"I will kill to change the world!"

THE GIN THIEF

ABOUT S.C. BARRUS

S.C. Barrus is the author/publisher of strange and thrilling adventure. His works include the novel *Discovering Aberration*, the serial *The Gin Thief,* and the short stories *The Peculiar Case of the Luminous Eye, Midway Between Heaven & Hell*, and *The Hanging Gardens.*

SIGN UP FOR OUR MONTHLY GIVEAWAY

Visit **AwayAndAway.com/Giveaway** to enter one of the monthly book giveaways sponsored by Away & Away Publishing and S.C. Barrus.

DISCOVERING ABERRATION
BY S.C. BARRUS

Readers Say:

"A wonderful and exciting adventure, with dark and strange places so greatly detailed and characters with depth and personality. Read this book! It will truly leave you wanting more!"

-Maria Schillaci

"I loved this book! Aside from it being a truly intriguing story of adventure, mystery, and high technology with enough action to keep me turning pages as fast as I could read...I was enthralled by the word choice and mastery of composition."

-Richard Jones

"This is kind of a steampunk version of Indiana Jones, and good, pure steampunk."

-Peter Henderson

www.ingramcontent.com/pod-product-compliance
Lightning Source LLC
Chambersburg PA
CBHW020411150626
46554CB00013B/666